I0450835

The Malacca Umbrella

The Eneko Sora detective series, Volume 2

David Scurlock

Published by Yama publishing, 2025.

THE MALACCA UMBRELLA

First edition. January 31, 2025.

Copyright © 2025 David Scurlock.

ISBN: 978-1738469727

Written by David Scurlock.

Also by David Scurlock

The Eneko Sora detective series
The Malacca Umbrella
The Spanish Connection

Standalone
The Missing Samurai Sword

Watch for more at www.yamapublishing.com.

Table of Contents

My heartfelt thanks to my daughter, Jenny who helped edit the manuscript. And a big thank you to Stephen Hearst, who came up with some brilliant designs for the book cover.

Chapter 1—The Girls are back

George was hanging from the rafters, naked, kicking and swearing at her captors, and screaming, "Eneko." I was trying to reach out to her, but I was being held back. I awoke in a sweat.

Again, I heard my name being called. I threw on some clothes and went through to the office. George looked in fine form. Her hair was longer; it seemed even more luxurious. The Spanish sunshine had brought out her freckles. She looked radiant—no bruises, even leaner and fitter. She threw her arms around me, kissed me on the lips for a long time, then slapped me on my rear. "Bamboo cane, eh?"

I laughed.

She laughed, threw off her coat, and said, "What's happening? Anything for me to do?"

"Loads, but it can wait. Tell me about your holiday?"

"Eneko, it was wonderful. After Rhian gave us the-all clear and we didn't look like a pair of female boxers, we drove to London and then by train to Paris. Paris was wonderful. Spring was in the air, and you know what they say... The place has a real atmosphere; we did a lot: the Champs-Élysées, the Eiffel Tower, Notre Dame, the Arc de Triomphe, and Les Halles. I walked my legs off. Bee was in her element. Her fluent French got the locals on our side. We splurged on clothing, and I have changed. Just wait and see. People in the street were, well, very French. I loved the pavement cafes and the art museums."

"Then on to Barcelona and the Costa Brava by train. The scenery was green, unspoilt in France, and muted. Barcelona was bustling, but edgy. The police and the Guardia Civil were everywhere. Bee had rented a cottage from a family friend near the beach in Sitges, and we went swimming every day. After a few dips, the bruising disappeared, and I felt like a new woman. Bee swims like a fish, so we stayed in the sea for hours each day. We even played water polo with some of the teenage sons of the fishermen. It was brilliant. We used to get up early

1

in the mornings, swim, and then return to eat and drink pastis and sardines with the fishermen. What a way to start the day. We had a cleaner, and she saw us in bed. She never even blinked. Her husband was one of the fishermen, but nobody said anything, and we lived like one family. I love Spain. Why don't we open an office there?"

"Slow down. Did you stay on the Costa Brava all the time?"

"Yes, twenty-three glorious days. Then we took a bus up to Bilbao to see Bee's family for a couple of days and then train, train, and train back to Liverpool. I owe you big time, boss."

Before I could reply, Begonia walked in; she too looked sensational, tanned, fit, and with a healthy glow. Her hair cascaded down past her waist. She flung her arms around me and kissed me on the lips, the cheeks, and the forehead. "Have I forgotten anywhere?" The girls laughed.

"You're both crazy, you know."

"Crazy about you, they cooed?"

I laughed. "Well-rehearsed. So, Begonia, what are you going to do now?"

Begonia said, "Dear Eneko, you are now looking at Pedro Bengoa's new personal assistant. He got in touch and asked if I would like the job. His secretary, Joyce, is retiring and moving to Scotland."

"Wow, that's great! You're the perfect choice. Why didn't I think of that?"

"I'm off to work as soon as I've got changed. And as today is Friday, I think we should celebrate, and Rhian is coming up to town, too. Can't wait."

George looked at me. "We need to talk."

George and Begonia nipped up to George's place and got changed into work clothes, George into a flattering black, tight skirt, and a white blouse with three-quarter-length sleeves. I started sorting out cases. George grabbed the mail and put things into work order. I went to get changed, and as I was coming back, I could hear the typewriter and the phone going. Thank God George was back.

George said, "Hang on a mo," to someone on the phone, and passed it over to me. The dulcet tones of Sugar came down the line. "15 minutes in the White Star for a quick half?"

"Right, see you there."

"George, if you need me, I'll be in the White Star." She nodded over the typewriter.

I walked up the lane. Spring was in the air. George had brought the pleasant weather with her. The sun had a bit of warmth, the air seemed fresher, the tang of the sea smelled good, and even the cobbles looked cleaner. Young Eric, one of Frank's party-time urchins at the cooper's yard, yelled, "Hiya Eneko, your Land Rover needs a clean." I threw him the keys, "When you've finished, give the keys to Frank, all right?" He raced off, his skinny legs going like the clappers.

I entered the pub, and Sugar waltzed in, looking fine in a navy-blue suit and a Lancashire Cricket tie.

I said, "Am I looking at the new Chief Inspector? Or just a pay rise?"

"You're in big trouble, mate."

"Why?"

"The chief wants to know why there are no new dead bodies turning up or drug villains getting arrested?"

"Ah! Is your star on the wane, lad?"

"He said it's no fun right now. Can you believe it? Mr Peace & Bloody Quiet wants some action!"

"So, you want me to shoot somebody?"

"Only if he's a known drug dealer, trafficker, or gun runner."

"That shouldn't be too hard in this town. Mind you, George is back, so anything could happen. Trouble follows her like a shadow."

"You'll be able to get some things done now that the boss is back, eh?"

"I must admit it has been peaceful, but I'm sure it'll pick up."

Maisy came over with the beer. "Sorry for the delay lads; the gaffer was just changing the barrel."

"Since you're leading the quiet life, mate, the lasses in the pool will be heartbroken!"

"Au contraire, my love life is at an ebb. And if I don't get wed to Sarah soon, she'll do me in one night when I'm asleep. She's warned me: no more playing away, or I could end up with nothing to play away with. She's becoming a ruthless lady."

"Not before time, Sugar, me old mate. I'm amazed she's put up with you for so long. Must be love?"

"I know, now that it's talk of kids, which is fine, but I know that's the end of my philandering. Then it's pipe and slipper time, and me getting my jollies by putting the villains behind bars."

"Jesus, Sugar, they'll be queuing up to leave. Leave a few for me, mate. Got to make a living!"

"Anyway, I'm here to let you know the word is there's something big in the offing. A load of bloody villains from the smoke are up in our patch, so keep your ears peeled! I'll keep you posted if I hear anything. Got to go, busy day with the boss, and later Sarah's got me going to the flics tonight!"

I walked up the street, people watching: the trams were still clunking past, the ladies were out in force, shopping or grabbing lunch. Skirts seemed to be the order of the day, with tight blouses and short jackets, some topped off with a beret. It looked good, and spring-like. I nipped into Rushworths, and Michael had got me a copy of Stéphane Grappelli and Django Reinhardt playing with the "English Quintette," recorded in London in 1946. I was dying to listen to it. Elated, I meandered up to the Kardomah through a throng of people, all enjoying the fine spring weather and clean air. The winter had been terrible, incessant smog had made the city a grubby, sooty disaster. But now nobody remembered. The power of the sun was a miracle worker! I walked into the Kardomah, and Ruby, my favourite waitress, still sporting her beehive hairdo, pointed me to a table in the corner. I sat down, and my coffee arrived. "Alright En? When's George getting back? I haven't seen her for yonks."

"She got back this morning, typing away like a good 'un."

"Tell her I said hi."

It was marvellous to see the girls back safe and sound. They both seemed to have recovered from the beating they got during The Missing Samurai Sword case. I hoped that there would be no lasting psychological effects. The girls were battered black and blue, but thanks to Rhian's doctoring skills and some Mediterranean cuisine and Spanish sunshine, they looked so much better. That case had been brutal for all of us. The mob from London and Mansell had murdered Charlotte over drugs, money, and power. Binns, my erstwhile silent partner, and I had obliterated the gang, but not before Charlotte had died an awful death in the quicksand at the river Dee. George and Begonia had been fortunate. Rabbit, Binns's right-hand man, got the message through to us, and we rescued the girls. Binns and I had come out smelling of roses, both unscathed and, as a bonus, with a considerable amount of cash. The police, in the shape of Sugar, had been one step behind us, but the top brass were well pleased.

To clear the head, I took a walk down to the Pier Head and watched the ships and ferries ply their trade. I loved the floating landing stage. It brought you so close to the water, even if the water was a dark-grey colour. I took the ferry to Woodside and looked back at the Liver Buildings. They were impressive, but the sunlight showed how the fog and smog had blackened them. On the return journey, the crew was expressing their despair over the obvious conclusion: Liverpool was going to be relegated this year. That brought back memories of my dad and me standing on the Anfield Road end, cheering the lads on. Even though my father was Spanish, and my mother was Chilean and half Japanese, I was a born and bred Scouser. I belonged in this city, and apart from my time working as a war correspondent during the civil war in Spain and WW2 and studying in Japan, this was home.

Back at the Pier Head, I jumped on the Dockers Umbrella and took it to the Dingle. Then I traipsed along the Cassy, but not for long as the tide was on the turn, so I didn't explore the many caves. The river was teeming with ships, with trade coming and going to all four corners of the world. Liverpool was a major player in shipping, but for how much longer? I wondered. I took the tram back to the Pier Head and wandered up to Philipson & Nephew on Victoria Street to pick up a copy of 'The Hobbit' by Tolkien. Begonia would love it, as she was a real literary buff. The shop was the same as ever: busy. After waiting in a line for a while, I got served and took my book home with me. The sky looked ominous, but so far, no rain as I walked back to the office. George was still typing away, so I made some coffee and lit up two Passing Clouds. George stopped typing. "Boss, we've got a lot of catching up to do."

"You're not wrong, but let's stop for today and enjoy the evening before the work gets crazy."

George packed up for the day and went for a shower and to change before Begonia got back. The evening came with a real downpour. Begonia and George popped round. Rhian was a no-show; she was stuck at work all weekend, so we stayed in. Begonia surprised me by making a tortilla Española with some chorizo she'd brought back from Spain and some excellent Rioja. We ate, drank, and caught up on what had been going on. Begonia presented me with a red Basque beret and a grey one as well. Chuffed, I felt even better when she opened the book I'd bought her. She yelled with delight. Their newfound energy was infectious. The experience in Wales and their holiday in Europe had changed them. Their eyes said it. George radiated confidence and determination. We went to bed after I drank too much Rioja and too much Remy. George said she'd be in the office in the morning, as she had loads of work to catch up on, and Begonia said she had a load of work to catch up on for Senor Bengoa as well. On Saturday, I thought these girls were keen.

Chapter 2—A Ridiculous story

I was in a state of bliss. George felt so close, trapped in my embrace, kissing me, and rubbing my shoulder. "Eneko, it's 10:30, and what are you dreaming about? Time for a bath—a cold one, mister.

I opened my eyes. George was looking at me with amusement on her lips and in her eyes, dressed for the office. She opened the taps in the bath, and with a "Coffee in 10 minutes," she was gone. I showered, shaved, and then plunged in. The cold hit me hard, but it got rid of my headache and got my brain working. I dressed in cords, a roll-neck sweater, and moccasins and headed into the office. George was typing. The smell of brewed coffee greeted me. I made two cups and handed one to George.

"Are you okay, Boss?" She said, lighting a couple of Passing Clouds. I mumbled, "Uh, huh." We drank and smoked in silence.

Before I could say a word, George said, "You need breakfast. I'll get the bacon and eggs on the go. You manage the phone, okay?"

I sat down in her chair. George's body had left it with an aroma of "Tabu," the French perfume I'd introduced her to. It hung in the air like a permanent memory. George put the breakfast on the table and motioned for me to go over and eat. I sat down and ate my breakfast, followed by another cup of coffee. George was typing away ninety to the dozen. Her office skills had gone up a few notches since she started working. I sat in silence, my brain just about ticking over. I was admiring George's very French-looking office attire—a tight black skirt with a long slit at the back. The loud ringing of the phone broke my revelry.

George answered, "Just a moment, please." She looked over and mouthed, "Are you in?" I nodded. "Putting you through now, sir."

"Sora speaking."

"My name is Mr Daud. I was wondering if I could come and see you about a rather delicate matter. I'd prefer to talk about it face-to-face if that's not inconvenient?"

"Mr Daud, would sometime today be to your liking?"

"That would be perfect, Mr Sora. Should we say 1 pm at your office?"

"I'll be expecting you, Mr Daud."

George raised those eyebrows as only she could. "I'd better make you some more coffee, boss."

At 1 pm, Mr Daud entered the office. We shook hands, and George showed us to the comfortable couch and brought over a coffee. Mr Daud was a short, dapper man of about 60 with a weather-beaten look, calm eyes, and a deadpan expression on his face. I thought he looked Malaysian, or Indonesian. I gave him my best smile and passed the sugar.

"Mr Sora, what I am about to convey sounds like a fairy tale of times past, and it's true it has that form. But it's all happening now and has the possibility of exploding into violence. My master, who is no longer with us, had three daughters, one of whom would take charge of things when he died. He was the leader of a small fiefdom in eastern Indonesia, but one that was rich in minerals, timber, and oil. It is also active in merchant shipping around the world. My master could not decide which of his three daughters would inherit the title, as it's passed down to the oldest son, but in this case, there is none. So, my master had this idea of setting a puzzle for his daughters, and the one who solved it would inherit the title. He had the whole thing drawn up, and I and four other judges would decide on the validity of each candidate. Are you following my gist, Mr Sora?"

"Yes, so far, Mr Daud."

"Good, because this is where it gets a little tricky. My master was a huge fan of Agatha Christie and her novels, especially those that featured Hercule Poirot. He devised a plot that they would have to solve to become the leader. The holder of the office wears a gold chain with various jewels, but the most striking part is a huge, red ruby that sits in the middle of the chain of office. This ruby hid in a port somewhere in the world—there were several simple clues, but the most difficult one was that the daughters could only travel by sea and could not use passports. The daughter who found the ruby and returned to the fiefdom would inherit the title."

"I thought only one daughter would attempt the puzzle, as it would take some time—but I was mistaken. The clues were simple: the ruby lies beneath the bird that guards the river. It never flies, gets wet, or gets lost. As you can see, Mr Sora, a strange story, but one that requires a certain determination to see it through. The daughters are Jannah, Mira, and Jasmin. These are their photographs, and as you can see, they are desirable women, all unmarried but with playboys and philanderers who wish to marry them and become the new leader through marriage. A genuine test for Poirot, don't you think?"

I looked at the photographs. The women were young and beautiful, and they would be a catch for any future husbands.

"But why do you think the trail leads to Liverpool?" I asked.

"Ah! Mr Sora, please take a few days to think it over, and then contact me at the Adelphi."

I smiled and said I'd contact him at the Adelphi.

Chapter 3—George the sharpshooter

George had been earwigging our conversation and looked at me after Mr Daud had left. "Wow! What a crazy dad, sends his girls on a find-the-parcel game, brilliant. Sounds like something my dad would have dreamed up."

"Your dad?"

"Yeah, when I was about 13, he hid a sniper rifle. I had to find out if I wanted to use it in the finals in north Wales."

"A sniper rifle?"

"Yeah, I was the Welsh junior target rifle champion."

"Well, it's not something to bring up in polite conversation, is it?"

"Yeah, I'd like to know. How good are you?"

"I can hit anything up to 600 yards."

"What rifle do you use?"

"Now I use my very own Mosin-Nagant sniper rifle. One of dad's mates picked it up during the war."

"Bloody Hell, George, where do you go shooting?"

"It's been awhile but over near Binns's place."

I looked at her. Nothing surprised me anymore about George. I just laughed and said, "Let's have a drink and a natter. I've got something to say."

George said, "So have I."

George made the coffee and did her usual thing with the fags, and I poured the Remy.

"George, I want you to become my partner."

"Boss, I thought you'd never ask! But can Bee stay as well?"

I looked at her, then she started laughing, "Your face, boss."

I gave George my pissed off look. She grabbed my arm, kissed me on the cheek, "Sorry best behaviour, promise."

"George, I need a partner in this detective agency, one I can trust and get along with. We are expanding and you are also better than me at digging up facts and you're clever, learn fast and very tough."

George beamed at me.

"You know I've been dreaming you'd say that, but on one condition, teach me how to fight. I've often wondered how you stopped those local scum bags beating me up in the street before we'd even met. But then I saw you first hand dismantle those bastards in Charlotte's place in Wales and I never want to be in that situation again without being able to defend myself. Even old Bernie said you were an absolute dynamite street fighter."

She looked very determined and much stronger and surer of herself than when we met.

"Okay, but it's difficult. You'll get plenty of bruises."

"Not a problem. I surprised myself at how much better and quicker I got at swimming in Spain. I even did some running, Bee thought I'd lost the plot. But if I'm a partner, I want to help when the going gets rough, okay? And I'll teach you how to use a rifle. You can borrow one off Binns. He has got a couple like mine."

"George, fighting is hard work. It takes dedication and practice—daily. If you honestly want to do it, I'll teach you, but I have warned you."

"Boss, I never want to be in that position again without having the skills to deal with it."

"Okay, I understand that."

"One more thing, boss, that's been intriguing me for ages. Quite a few times I've come into the office early and checked to see if you were up and about and you weren't in, then an hour later you come out of your apartment, showered, and dressed. I won't tell anyone, but I know you're hiding something."

"Ah! Quite the detective!"

She smiled.

"Follow me, partner, but first close the office."

She followed me as I walked through my apartment to the hidden door and into the passageway that led to the end of the building, where a spiral staircase took you to the basement. George didn't utter a word as I showed her the gym. She looked at the floor to ceiling wine racks and the huge brandy barrels. I pressed a lever in one of the brandy barrels. It opened into another cellar where I kept my martial arts equipment and my collection of Kendo sticks, Samurai swords, and a shooting gallery. The shooting gallery was 6 ft wide and 180 ft long and lined with stone and the best soundproofing material I could find. George checked out my weapons: a Beretta 1934 from my days in Spain, a Browning Hi-Power, and a Colt M911A1 from an American friend in Japan. She asked me why I never ran out of cartridges, so I showed her how I manufacture my fresh rounds. George carried on her investigation for about 20 minutes, then nodded. We went back upstairs.

"Boss, I can't believe how organised you are. The basement is brilliant, and the hidden one is insane. I was going to suggest turning the empty storeroom upstairs into a gym, but there's no need!"

"No, we've got everything we need here, except the time and preparation to excel at fighting, but we'll work at it each day and you'll soon get strong and skilled, and bruised.

"I know and I'll keep this a secret from Bee. She'll only worry, anyway."

"George, she'll soon see the bruises. No way you can keep that from her."

"True boss, I just won't mention the swords or the guns."

"Another coffee, while I run the bath?"

"Do you mind if I join you? I'll get my things."

George shampooed her hair and washed herself. I noticed the nice all over-body-suntan. "I see you got a nice all-over tan."

"George laughed. It was so wonderful to swim and sunbathe with no clothes. I loved it, just like this bath."

"Okay, as you're relaxing, I've got a favour to ask. I want some information and advice from a Welsh lass who knows her way around the hills. When we were over at your place in Wales, Binns said that the cottage up above your place was for sale and it comes with a lot of land, those woods that cover the hillside. I'm thinking of buying it and getting the locals to graze their animals up there, cows, pigs, sheep. Binns said some locals and Rabbit would be up for it. No charge, just free grazing, maybe help get the local economy going. What do you think?"

"It's a superb idea, but it won't come cheap, you know. Leave it with me. I'll talk to the owner. You know, during the war, it was us land-girls that ran everything as all the men were away fighting. We took care of the farms, keeping the livestock healthy and maintaining the land. I used to take the animals up to the top grazing land in the summer, believe it or not, I used to run those hills as well. I was as fit as a fiddle. Then after the war some men came back, started working the land and the hills. But they were just going through the motions, looking back. Their wartime-experiences traumatised a lot of them, but we didn't realise it then. Some women lost the plot, too, and decamped to pastures new. So, it'll take a lot of hard work to get it back in shape, but with Binns and Rabbit in charge, they'll kick arse and get the lads and lasses going. And with Rhian and her vet's practice, it should all work out fine."

The doorbell rang. George got out of the bath and answered it. I heard laughter. "Bee wants to join us, boss."

"Okay, I called."

Begonia with her olive-skin complexion was a fair bit darker than George. Begonia washed and shampooed her hair and slid into the bath. I thought, what a way to spend Saturday afternoon bathing with two beautiful women.

Begonia said, "I love this bath. After bathing I feel so clean it's luxurious. Eneko, why don't you open a bathhouse for women? You'd make a fortune!"

George said, "Let's have a picnic. I've got most of the stuff at my place. Eneko's got the wine and the tele, job done, okay?"

We settled down to some home-cooked food, wine, and Remy. The conversion flowed only interrupted now and again by the latest new song on Radio Luxembourg. About 10 pm, the girls went to bed, and I turned in as well.

Chapter 4—George solves the riddle

Sunday morning: I got up around 7 am and did some work in the gym when the doorbell rang. George was there in shorts and a T-shirt.

"Bee is having a lie in. I fancy a workout, okay, boss?"

"Okay, let's do it."

George took to training like a veteran. She was tough, strong, and supple. I realised straight away that with proper planning and conditioning, she could develop into a real fighter. George lasted for about an hour, said I had knackered her, and went home for a shower. I also called it a day and took my time over a shower and dressed in my latest casual gear, perfect for a Sunday lunch, perhaps.

The doorbell rang, and the girls came in. "Eneko, we're starving. Any ideas?"

The girls looked elegant, black slacks and matching red sweaters under black duffle coats. Begonia's fashion sense was helping George. She looked the height of fashion.

I said, "Let's go out Heswall way. I'll get the car."

George said, "We won't fit in the Allard, boss."

"I've bought a Land Rover, got it while you were in Spain, lock up and I'll see you out front."

I nipped round to the coopers' yard and collected the Land Rover and drove around to the office. The girls climbed in. "This is brilliant," said George. "Can I drive back?"

"Yes, of course."

Spring was in the air at last, just a touch of mist to remind you warm weather was still a while away. The city centre looked closed for business, just some locals getting the Sunday papers. I smiled to myself. I loved having George and Begonia back. As we left the tunnel on the Birkenhead side, I noticed a Bentley changing lanes and keeping up with us. We drove on; the girls laughing and joking about how good they were at water polo, but only in the warm weather. We stopped at a pub that looked like a proper pub. The girls were in form and chatted about nothing and everything. I was getting a few looks from the local males who were admiring my lady friends, and some ladies were admiring the girls' fashion sense. The food arrived; it looked good. I excused myself and went into the gents. The Bentley that followed us was now parked at the end of the car park. Two men were sitting there, watching. As soon as I got back to the table, George slapped her hand on the table. "Got it."

"Got what?" said Begonia.

"Sorry, tell you both in the car."

Begonia looked at me and pointed to her head. I laughed. George stuck her tongue out at us and laughed, too.

We trooped out to the car, and I noted the number plate of our motor escort. Difficult to miss—an old blue Bentley! The journey back was uneventful, George refused to expand on her outburst in the car as she was driving, details to follow with a Remy was her reply. George parked the car in the cooper's yard, and we headed back to the office.

George put on my prized Italian Alfonso Bialetti coffee maker to prepare our afternoon coffee. Begonia armed herself with three glasses and a bottle of Remy. George placed the coffeepot on the table and Begonia served. We both eyed George.

"Okay, you know that clue that Mr Daud gave us? I've solved it, it's easy, so it must be a put-on."

"How come?"

"Mr Daud said, the ruby lies beneath the bird that guards the river, never flies, nor gets wet, or ever gets lost."

"So," I said!

"The Liver Bird guards the river, never flies. Beneath the Liver Bird is the Liver Building. The ruby never gets lost, so it's in the lost property office and inside an umbrella so it doesn't get wet."

Begonia looked at me. "George, that's astonishing, just like Sherlock Holmes, don't you think, Eneko?"

"Before you thank me for my brilliant deduction, maybe it's so obvious that everyone has thought of it."

I said, "Don't sell yourself short, George. It hadn't occurred to me, and I know the city well. How do you know there's a lost property office there?"

"Because I lost an umbrella on the ferry once and a sailor told me that's where they got deposited and he was right, my brolly was there."

Begonia said, "Eneko is right, George, most Liverpudlians wouldn't know that, so why would three girls from Indonesia know?"

"They wouldn't, but they could employ people to find out. We're talking about a huge amount of money and power. And why is Mr Daud here in Liverpool?"

"That's a good point, George. When we were on the way to the pub, I spotted a car following us. It stayed in the car park and followed us back here, not to the office but to Liverpool. I'll get Sugar to find the owner of the car tomorrow and set up a chat with Mr Daud."

Chapter 5—The proper story

The next day I rang the Adelphi and spoke to Mr Daud and said I'd see him soon. George said she would ring Sugar and get the details about the car. I walked up to the Adelphi, such a refreshing spring day. There was still a slight haze, but the sun was going to burn that off by the afternoon. As I was going to the Adelphi, I dressed for the occasion in a navy-blue corduroy suit, white shirt, and dark brown brogues, and a matching scarf. The weather put a spring in my step, and I arrived in a cheerful mood. Mr Daud was waiting for me in the tearoom. We shook hands, and he signalled to the waitress, who looked charming with her lace cap which topped off the uniform. She nodded and went to carry out the order.

Mr Daud thanked me for coming and asked me what I thought about his story.

I said, "It appears on face value to be fanciful and melodramatic, but not implausible."

"Ah! So, you have some ideas about the clues?"

"I do, but first please explain why your employer chose Liverpool as the backdrop to this adventure?"

"I can see you're astute, Mr Sora. My master chose this fine city because, as a young man, he sailed to this port many times and enjoyed its sights and its people. He once told me he felt at home in Liverpool, he felt respected."

"You mentioned your surprise that the three daughters would try to find the ruby. Why?"

"I failed to consider how much the possibility of wealth and power can cloud one's moral compass. But how to resolve it is the key question now."

"I'm still a little confused about how you think or want this matter resolved."

"How very perceptive of you, Mr Sora. I'll put my cards on the table and my loyalties, too. In our little fiefdom, only the youngest daughter, Jasmin, has any popularity as she came home to look after her father. The other two daughters flaunt their wealth and notoriety through association with playboys and other scandalous types. My master knew if either of the elder daughters took power, the region could erupt in flames, whereas he knows Jasmin is a true democrat and wants the people to hold the power, not an omnipotent ruler. It's time for us to make a peaceful change before a violent one hits us."

"So, Mr Daud, do you know where the ruby is?"

"No, I'm not sure. All I have is an idea, or a name. Agatha Christie, I'm sure, is the clue."

"Okay, Mr Daud, leave it with me. One last question, are you assisting Jasmin and where are the daughters now?"

"Clearly, I want Jasmin to find the ruby as I trust my master in all matters. To answer the second part of the question, Jasmin is on her way to Liverpool and her sisters, I think, are in London arranging teams to locate the missing item."

"Why don't Jannah and Mira join forces?"

"Because they dislike each other."

"I'll be in touch when I know something definite, Mr Daud."

We shook hands, and I made my way back to the office. This plot or puzzle seemed much too simple to me, but I was sure there would be many twists and turns before long.

Chapter 6—Bernie is a gem

George was brewing up as I arrived. I sat down, George prepared the cigarettes, and we smoked and drank in silence. George raised her eyebrows, and I took a deep breath.

"We have an actual situation here, George. But that said I've got an idea that may work, you've solved the location of the ruby and now I think I've got a name for the lost property office. I want you to pose as a niece of Miss A Christie. You've come to the lost property office to recover your aunt's umbrella. I'm pretty sure it'll have her name embossed on the handle, so it shouldn't present a problem. If it does, we'll have to think again."

"Okay, boss, should I walk down now?"

"I'll walk with you—just give me a minute."

"Do I get to carry a gun, too, boss?"

"No, you get to carry the umbrella. Oh, and what did Sugar say?"

"He'll let us know later today."

I pocketed my Beretta as we headed for the Pier Head and the Liver Building. George's suntan and her new fashion sense stressed her athletic appearance. As we strolled along, I glanced into a couple of shop windows to see if we were being followed. Something jarred as we walked through town, so I got hold of George's hand and took a turn onto North John Street and headed into Watson and Prickard.

George smiled. "Are you buying me some more lingerie, darling? "

I said, "Why not? Have a chat with Lavina and I'll just browse for a while."

"Must be the sunshine putting you in a buying mood, boss?"

"Get lost."

While George chatted to Lavina, I positioned myself so I could see who was coming into the shop or dawdling outside. We were being followed by at least three, two men and a woman. This was going to be tricky. Lavina waved and she and George went off to look at the underwear. I went upstairs and entered the office and waved at the girls and asked if I could use the phone. Begonia answered the phone at her office. In Basque, I explained the situation.

"Begonia, can you go to the lost property office and pick up the umbrella—in the name of Mrs A Christie? Then nip into the ladies, unscrew the handle, and take out the stone. Take the umbrella back to the lost property office. And tell them the umbrella was too unwieldy, and could you leave it for a few more days?"

"Okay, Eneko, then what do I do?"

"Walk up to Watson and Prickard and join George in choosing some underwear."

I waited, trying not to let my impatience show, looking out of the windows, trying to glimpse Begonia. At last, she came into the shop, saw me, kissed me, left a little something in my pocket and then went off with the girls. I went outside, caught a passing taxi, and headed uptown. My followers were too late grabbing a cab, so I lost them. I got out at Central Station and then made sure no one was following me as I made my way to Bernie Goldstein's office.

Bernie's secretary showed me to this office.

Bernie said, "This is a pleasant surprise," and shook my hand with feeling.

I said, "Bernie I need a big favour, and it needs to be done quickly and in secret."

"Well, that's the best request I've had in a long time. What's it all about?"

I put the ruby on the desk in front of him.

"Jesus Eneko, do you know what this is worth?"

I said, "No idea, but that's not what I've come about. I need a copy, one that could fool someone for a while."

Bernie blinked, raised his eyebrows, whistled, and said, "It can be done, but dark red rubies are difficult."

I said, "I need it done yesterday, though, and don't worry about the cost."

"Okay, Eneko, do you remember Moshe? He's a master at making glass look like the real thing. I'll get him on it today. He owes you a favour, so don't worry."

"Bernie, this is potentially dangerous, so when it's complete, call me and I'll meet you here to pick it up, okay?"

"No problem, give me 48 hours."

I left the office, walked to Central Station, caught a cab, and went back to meet up with the girls. They were talking with Lavina when I arrived. I paid the bill and Begonia went back to work and George and I headed back to the office. George said she wanted to work out and try out some new moves. So, we headed down to the gym. George went through her new routine. She was gaining strength in a hurry. And her power and suppleness were impressive. It wouldn't be long before she was a formidable fighter.

"Boss, Bee has brought me up to speed on what happened at the lost property office. She was ecstatic she did the job without cocking it up."

She'll be around after work for a bath and to try on her new underwear.

"Boss, can we have a go with the pistols, please?"

I looked at her. "Sure, let's see how accurate you are."

I gave her the Beretta, explained the rudiments of the action, recoil and sighting. She picked it up, unloaded it, loaded it, and checked the safety catch. Then took it to bits and put it back together with speed and efficiency. After checking the magazine, she aimed and fired without hesitation. She smiled, reloaded, and then fired more rapidly. The shots all hit the centre of the target, excellent shooting for a so-called beginner.

She smiled, "Not just a pretty face, boss. I'll nip upstairs and put the bath on while you finish up."

I worked out for a while, finished up and went upstairs. George was already in the bath when Begonia arrived. I shut the office and took a shower and left the girls to it. Then I got dressed and went into the apartment. The girls were already there — "lingerie modelling time boss," said George. They tried on their underwear, they looked terrific. Begonia's a little more revealing than George's, but excellent choices. Begonia reached out and smacked George's thigh. "Eneko, George has more muscles every day. I'm going to train as well. She makes me look puny."

I said, "As much as I'd like to see you girls in a state of near nudity all night, we need to go over our new plan."

George said, "Right, I'll put the coffee on. Bee, can you get the Remy? And, boss, can you get your pen and paper ready?"

"Okay girls, this is what we've got: an umbrella, a ruby which is now being copied as we speak; a gang trailing George and me, and the two elder sisters up to no good. And not forgetting that Jasmin is about to arrive in Liverpool and hoping to find the ruby so she can take up her inheritance."

Begonia said, "Are you sure Mr Daud is totally honest, particularly about Jasmin being a true democrat?"

"I agree with Bee, boss—isn't she just too good to be true?"

"You could be both correct, but until we learn otherwise, let's stick with the plan. We'll put the fake ruby back in the umbrella, only we know about that. It's our insurance against a major cock up. We need to distract the clerk while we replace the ruby in the umbrella. "

"How, boss?"

"Not sure yet, but we'll think of something. To be honest, I'm more worried about the people that are following us. We could end up with two different groups on our tail."

"When will the copy be ready, boss?"

"Bernie said it would be ready in a couple of days. So, in the interim, make sure you keep a low profile when you're out and about."

"Okay, boss, see you in the morning."

The girls left, and I sat down with a Remy and tried to put all the evidence into place. I was sure that things were going to get ugly. People who hired gangs had money and influence. Time for a battle plan: I rang Binns and said I'd see him for lunch in the White Star.

In the morning, George arrived at 7 am for her workout. She was improving at a phenomenal rate. Her suppleness, speed, and power were tremendous. George was typing away when I got up to the office and the coffee was on the go. The phone rang. George answered, pursed her lips, and whistled.

"Boss, Sugar said that the vehicle is owned by a company in London. It looks like it's a front and it's a front for a gang specialising in everything from jewellery theft to drugs and kidnapping."

"We need to be on the ball, George. I think this case is going to become violent."

"So, my training may come in useful, then."

"Pour the coffee and let's get thinking."

Chapter 7—The landowner

After coffee, George got on with her typing and I ran through how this saga could pan out. I was seeing Binns for lunch, so a quick chat with Mr Daud was in order. The receptionist at the Adelphi said he had gone to the docks, as he booked a taxi to go to Sandon Dock. I wondered if he was meeting Jasmin and if so, where would they go. It would be stupid to stay at the Adelphi in plain sight.

The phone rang, and George started a conversation in Welsh, a very animated conversation. She ended it and jumped up, hugged me, and gave me a big kiss.

"Boss, you're the new owner of a rather large amount of land, mostly covered in trees. The landowner and his neighbour on the other side of the valley have joined forces and done a deal—you now own the lot. It comes with two cottages, four barns, and two storehouses."

"Jesus! George, can I afford it?"

"It's all yours for £17,500, which is highway robbery. He only sold it to you because of your welsh connections—me."

"Wow, I'm seeing Binns in the White Star for a pint. I wonder what he'll think?"

"Boss, he'll be over the moon. He's got lots of plans, you know. Can I come with you to the pub?"

"Partner, you certainly can."

The White Star was open for business, the whiff of Brasso and furniture polish was in the air. The copper and brass wore a dazzling sheen. Maisy was serving Binns and gave us a big smile.

"Blimey Eneko, buying the staff lunch. It really must be spring."

"Morning Maisy, as Binns is in the chair, I'll have the usual plus three ploughman's lunches and whatever George is drinking."

Binns and I left Maisy and George at the bar and went and sat over by the fireplace. I brought Binns up to speed with the latest developments and my concerns.

He stroked his chin. "It sounds like it could get messy. I'll do a recce on the car and the gang's modus operandi."

That from a man who always dressed like the next war was about to start spoke volumes. George came over with Maisy in attendance with the lunches and sat down.

"Excuse me boss," then she broke into Welsh for about 5 minutes. Binns smiled, looked at me, and winked.

Binns lent over and slapped me on the shoulder.

"Eneko, that's superb news—it couldn't have come at a better time. You realise you're about to push start a cottage industry: meat, cheese, butter, milk. And wool and leather for clothes, etc. The land up there will support a lot of animals and, of course, families. I can't wait to get things organised with Rabbit. This is right up his street. That expansion will go grand with my bit of investment up there, God! It'll really change things for the better."

"Well, let's hope we don't have to take refuge up there from these mobsters, who seem to head our way. Mr Daud has gone to pick Jasmin up and take her, I assume, to a house he's rented out. Tomorrow if I get the ruby back from Bernie, we'll do the swop at the lost property office. George and I will make up some cock and bull story, enough time for Begonia to make the swap and then get the hell out of the way. But I think we're going to need some backup from you, mate, as I'm worried about the number of people we have tailing us."

"Okay, I'll stay outside under cover and try to get a clear picture of who is who. And I'll be on hand if anything kicks off."

George said, "That sounds like a plan, boss. We need to get as much information as possible about these gangs."

"Okay, I'll try to catch up with Mr Daud later today and see what he's doing. Jasmin may have some information for us that could be very useful. I'll call you as soon as I know what time tomorrow so we can get organised."

Lunch finished, the conversation turned back to Wales and how we were going to start a mini-cottage-industry boom. Binns said the price was right, and the property had a lot of land. The land had tree cover, excellent prime land for our ideas. He also mentioned that in the long distant past, they had found gold in the streams. I somehow couldn't imagine us sluicing for gold in the hills, but never say never. We left the White Star, George, to do some more office work—I'd hang around for Mr Daud to surface. I lit a couple of Passing Cloud, gave one to George, and brewed up some coffee.

"George, tomorrow at the lost property office, you get Begonia to faint. The clerk will come to help you, and I'll slip the ruby back in its rightful place, simple but effective."

"Why will the clerk help?"

"Two beautiful women in distress. Are you kidding?"

The phone started ringing. George answered, "Good morning, George speaking, Mr Sora's secretary Yes, Mr Daud, I'll put him on."

I wrote partner, not secretary, on a piece of paper, passed it to George and said, "Hello Mr Daud, how are you?"

"I'm fine now that Jasmin has arrived safely. We would like to have a meeting as soon as possible. I have rented a house near Calderstones Park. Could we meet in the park at the old oak tree tomorrow morning at 10 am?"

"Certainly, but why the subterfuge?"

"Ah! Mr Sora, I'll explain when we meet."

"See you tomorrow, Mr Daud."

George laughed, "Okay partner, more coffee?"

"Yeah, please."

"What are we going to name the agency, boss?"

"No idea, Passing Cloud, passing thoughts, passing by."

"Jesus! boss, they're awful! I'll work on it, maybe get Bee to give me a hand."

"Mr Daud really knows his local geography. How the hell does he know about the old oak tree in Calderstones Park?"

"Okay partner, we sound like a western movie!"

Chapter 8—Who's following who?

Time to get some fresh air, so I walked down to the overhead railway and took my usual ride to the Dingle. Knackered looking dockers on the train with woodbines on the go were heading home after another long shift. Getting off the Overhead at the Dingle underground station which always struck me as incongruous, I walked up and along the Cast Iron Shore. Old Holborn pipe tobacco smoke wafted past as I traipsed the well-trodden path. Overhead, swooping gulls were making a racket, almost drowning out the distant horns of the ships as they seeped upstream. From my position on the shore, I could see right across the river. Its dark grey appearance was not an enticing sight. As I walked past Aigburth bus station, I thought I glimpsed somebody following me. I crossed the road and made my way up Lark Lane and into Sefton Park. I picked out two following me on foot and maybe another in a car crawling along. A cab appeared, so I flagged it down and asked him to go to the Adelphi Hotel. The cabbie sped off, and I spotted my tail climb into the car that had been crawling along before they followed my cab. At the Adelphi, I got out, paid the driver, and went into the hotel and headed for the bar. I ordered a drink, borrowed a newspaper, and dawdled. I didn't see anyone follow me into the hotel. So, after a while, I got up and left by the side entrance, cut down the back of Lime Street, and headed back to the office.

"Enjoy your walk, boss, I mean Eneko?"

"Yes, but three people followed me."

George gave me a quizzical look, and before I could answer, the phone rang.

"Mr Sora's partner, George speaking, how can I help? Oh, hi Binns, yeah, I'll put him on." She winked as she passed me the phone.

"Eneko, did you spot they followed you to the Dingle?"

"I spotted the three of them. That's why I went into the park."

"Yeah, two on shanks's pony and one driver, but did you spot the other motor with three handsome looking chaps in it?"

"No, I didn't. I'm meeting Mr Daud and Jasmin tomorrow in Calderstones Park in front of the old oak tree at 10 am. Can you act as my spotter in case I'm followed?"

"I've got photos of all of them and the car registrations as well. But make sure you take a taxi and get out at Calder Girls High School and cut through the park to the bandstand. I'll be under cover, but don't worry, I've got a gun."

"Okay, see you tomorrow or not."

The phone rang. George answered and gave it to me.

Bernie was on the line. Hi Eneko, "Moshe has done the job, it looks an excellent copy. And as it's you, he's made two for the price of one."

"That's brilliant Bernie. Can I pick them up after lunch at your place?"

"Perfect, I'll get them gift wrapped."

George said, "Did I hear right? He's made two?"

"Yeah, you never know when the extra one could come in useful. What a day, I've had enough for today. I'm going to put the bath on. You can join me if you have time?"

"I'm meeting Bee at the Kardomah at 6:00 pm. It'll give enough time to indulge in a luxurious bath before meeting Bee. I'll just get a change of gear."

I gave George the once over at bath time. She was looking more muscular by the minute and more confident. She left the bath first and dashed off to meet Begonia while I let the hot water smooth the kinks out of my body and massage my troubled mind. Tomorrow, we'd all have to be careful, and George was going to have to keep a close eye on Begonia in case the gangs spotted her. I got dressed and went downstairs and made sure my weapons were all in order. I made a quick call to Binns and mentioned weapons. He said he'd already got his gear together, and he'd give me the film to develop so we could put names to faces. I decided on an early night, a Remy or two and some Stephane Grappelli, to clear the head.

In the morning, I was about to go down to the gym when I heard George open the office door.

"Can I join you downstairs, boss?"

"Sure, you can, Partner," I replied.

George threw herself into training and put in some serious work with her kicks. I left her to it and after a quick shower went out into the office; the postman was at the door. He smiled and handed me a load of mail. I put it on George's desk and went and put the coffee on. George came upstairs, grabbed a coffee, and said, "See you in ten minutes."

I looked outside but couldn't see anyone loitering with intent, so I finished my coffee and waited for George. She came dashing into the office, fresh from her shower.

"That was a tough workout this morning, boss. Did you notice any improvement?"

"Yes partner, just keep at it and it will come. Practice makes it permanent and all that."

George started going through the post and I went through what was the order of the day. Binns was going to be the lookout at the park. I assumed Mr Daud and Jasmin would be easy to spot. A plan was taking shape in the back of my head.

"George, get your duffle coat and come with me this morning. You up for it?"

"Dead right, boss, I mean partner, er... Eneko."

"Okay, I don't think this will turn nasty, but better to be safe than sorry."

I handed her my Beretta. "Put that in your pocket and hopefully it'll stay there."

Chapter 9—The Scouser in Calderstones Park

George nodded and grabbed her coat, and we left, George putting up the 'Back later sign' on the front door. We walked along Victoria Street and hailed a cab. Spring sunshine was a bonus, flowers were blooming and may give us some cover in the park. The cabbie dropped us off at the bottom of Harthill Road. We entered the park and headed straight for the bandstand. The park was showing the birth of spring. Bluebells and crocus were popping out and trees were sprouting their leaves. George got hold of my hand and we walked down the path and across the grass towards the oak tree. In front of the oak, Mr Daud and a young lady were sitting on a bench. The young lady wasn't what I expected. Dressed in trousers, a polo-neck sweater, and a dark blue duffle coat, she looked the height of fashion. George caught my eye as we headed over to them. Binns would cover us, so I wasn't too worried.

Mr Daud stood up, "Good morning, Mr Sora, morning George, may I present Jasmin?"

"Isn't this place wonderful? I used to play here loads in spring and summer. It's still ace," Jasmin said.

I was sure I had a stunned expression on my face! So had George, by the look of her. Jasmin sounded like she was born and bred here.

George laughed and said, "Jasmin, tell me how you know the park and why do you talk like that? "

Jasmin took George by the arm, and they went for a stroll around the oak.

Mr Daud smiled and said, "Let's leave them to it. George will tell you the complete story when you get back to the office. We need to find the ruby before the other sisters arrive. They are the opposite of Jasmin; heartless. "

"Mr Daud, I found the ruby and I have a plan for you to return to your country with it. However, the ruby is not your biggest concern. We need to outfox your adversaries and make them believe they have won—not a straightforward task."

"I must admit, Eneko, that you are dead right. The sisters are travelling up from London, and both have a ruthless set of helpers to get the ruby and, I suspect, eliminate Jasmin. You were right in wondering why they didn't join forces, and I think they have, at least for the moment."

"Mr Daud, you are both in danger. Where are you staying, and do you have guards?"

"No, we're staying at an old friend's cottage in Green Lane, just down from the convent. Jasmin stayed there when she was at school here."

God! I thought, this is a mess. I said, "How did you get here? "

"We walked—it's just up the road."

I looked at him while I tried to think this through. Mr Daud was, as he said, his master's envoy. There didn't appear to be any real subterfuge about his method or his ideas, he seemed to be a man determined to look after his charge. But that didn't help, it just made me even more concerned for their safety. I thought thank God Binns was around.

I heard a rustle in the undergrowth. Binns's arm appeared signalled for us to join him at the park entrance by the school, so we followed him. Binns arrived in his Land Rover. We scrambled in, and without a word, he stepped on the accelerator, and we were off.

Binns said, "You were being followed. Any ideas where we should go?"

I said, "Your place now. Can you get in touch with Rabbit to sort out a hideout in the hills?"

"Yeah, no problem, I'll drop you two off at Penny Lane and then if they're still after me, I'll lose them before I get to my place."

I said, "This is Plan B, Mr Daud, but you'll be safe, and we'll be in touch later today, okay? "

"Yes, Mr Sora, that seems like an excellent plan."

George and I exited the Land Rover at Penny Lane. Jasmin waved, I waved back and realised I hadn't spoken a word to her! We went into Capaldi's coffee shop, they made the best coffee and served wonderful traditional Italian cakes. I looked out to see if any vehicles were following us. I spotted them as they slowed down for the corner. They appeared undecided, but then raced up the hill towards Picton Clock Tower. George looked at me and raised her eyebrows.

"Now what? "

I said, "Two coffees to start. "

The waitress heard me and smiled. "At the counter or near the window? "

I said, "Yeah, a table by the window would be fine. "

I said, "George, you start."

"Jasmin went to Calder. Can you believe it? Her father had an affair, and she was the result. Her mother died of natural causes a year later. Jasmin became the apple of her father's eye. Her father knew that if she got used to a royal household, she would understand nothing about real life. So, she went to stay with a family friend in Liverpool and she was enrolled in Calder Girls High School in 1937 and before that she attended Childwall Primary School for a couple of years. She's a real scouser!"

"But she must have missed her father?"

"I think he was overly protective of her safety even then. He used to visit now and again, and he was very pleased with her upbringing and her schooling. She made friends and nobody knew her real identity. She lived a normal childhood."

"Who did she stay with?"

"His ex-wife's elder sister, Grace, was married to a doctor, James Wilkie, and was brought up with them. Grace couldn't have children, so she was brought up as her daughter. Jasmin finished school and went to university in Glasgow to study medicine and after graduating, was going to work in Liverpool, but her father became ill, so she returned home to look after him. Her aunt and husband still live in Green Lane. That's where Jasmin has been staying."

"So where does Mr Daud stand in all this mystery?"

"He was the Sultan's private secretary, and he used to travel a lot on business so he would drop in and visit when he could. Nobody knew. It was difficult during the war, but he managed somehow, a very resourceful man! When Jasmin returned home to look after her father, as his doctor, she soon became popular. Her father was a revered leader with his opposition to the Japanese during the war. But now the title of Sultan is a misnomer as it no longer exists, but he still owns a huge amount of land and many business interests. His heir will be very wealthy indeed—we are talking millions."

"Jasmin looked after him until his death, then?"

"Yes, she used to ring Dr Wilkie if she needed help in her father's medical care. James and Grace Wilkie were great friends with the Sultan."

"Okay, let's keep that onboard and head back to the office and go through some ideas. This could get tricky."

I paid the bill, it had been a while since I'd been in Capaldi's, it hadn't changed. We grabbed a cab on Penny Lane and kept our thoughts to ourselves.

Chapter 10—Making plans

Back at the office, George settled down on the settee with pen and paper in hand and looked at me.

"Okay, boss, what do we know?"

"Okay, George. I'll list everything in chronological order, then we can start on what we don't know."

"Okay, this much we know: the ruby is under lock and key; Jasmin and Mr Daud are with Binns; Bernie has two copies for us; two gangs are after Jasmin and the ruby; we must exchange the ruby. What don't we know? The intentions of the gang; what they know; how many of them are there?

"Not very promising, boss."

"I know. They have the upper hand or, more likely, they think they do. Tomorrow we'll make the exchange at 1 pm. Phone Begonia and get her to meet you at the lost property office. I'll leave at 12 am. No doubt they'll follow me, but I'll lose them. Close the office and walk up to the Adelphi, go in, and then use the back exit, grab a cab and go to the Pier Head and get inside the lost property office and meet up with Begonia and wait for me."

"Okay boss."

"Right, let's put the weapons back and have a workout, go to dinner with Begonia, and have an early night."

Later in bed, my thoughts dwelled on tomorrow's plan. I had to make certain I lost the three trailing me, pick up the rubies and make sure the exchange went well in the lost property office.

In the morning, I rang Binns. Everything was fine. He was enjoying Jasmin's company. He reckoned she was more of a scouse than he was. Mr Daud had returned to the Adelphi to make the gang think Jasmin had not yet arrived. I somehow doubted that.

George was at her desk before me, catching up on some paperwork from the landowners in Wales. I put the coffee on and made some toast.

We drank and ate in our customary silence. George lit up a couple of Passing Clouds and passed one to me: "Where is this going with the exchange? We do it, then what?"

"Good question. Let's just take one step at a time. I've got a funny feeling things are going to be taken out of our hands. There are just too many imponderables."

"Terrific, apart from you sounding like you've swallowed the dictionary that tells me nothing."

George went back to work on the paperwork, and I rang Mr Daud, just to keep him in the picture and to see how he was faring. He sounded nervous, but in control. I explained what we were planning to do and told him I'd ring later to let him know the outcome. I rang Bernie and told him I'd be at his office at 12:30 pm. Bernie said he'd be waiting and everything was in order.

"Okay George, time to go. See you in about an hour."

"Okay boss."

We left together. I headed for Victoria Street and George walked up the lane in the tunnel's direction. On Victoria Street, I caught a cab and headed for Lewis's side entrance. I paid the cabbie and walked into the store, nipped down to the basement and exited into Central Station. I took a quick turn into Bold Street and dodged down a couple of back alleys and came out at the back of Bernie's shop.

He opened the door: "Morning Eneko, come right in." I followed and in the back room was a smiling Moshe.

"Morning Moshe, how are you?"

"I'm fine, Eneko" And he opened a silken bag with a drawstring and poured the contents out onto the table. "What do you think?"

I looked at all of them and they seemed identical to me. They all had the same colour, which left me dumbfounded. I said, "They look great, Moshe. How do I tell the difference?"

He laughed, "This one is the real one which he put into a smaller bag, and be careful because this quality, colour and size are rare, which means it's worth a small fortune."

"Moshe, you've done a brilliant job. How much do I owe you?"

He smiled, "For what? Making a couple of bits of glass. Please Eneko, don't be silly."

They both stood beaming at me. I shook both their hands and slipped out of the back door. I walked up the alley towards China Town and caught a cab to the Baltic Exchange. I walked into the bar, ordered a drink, and looked out of the window to check if anyone looked out of place. Nothing, just a bunch of regular customers enjoying a wet lunch. Outside, I hailed a cab, and we drove to the Cunard Building. The building looked quiet. Lunchtime, I supposed. In the building, I walked through the main lobby and downstairs to the lost property office. Begonia and George were waiting outside the door. I looked through the window and a lady was talking to the lost property man. She finished and came out. I signalled to George, and they went in. Begonia asked the man to check for a lost piece of luggage. As he checked, I came in. Begonia appeared to stagger and sink to the ground.

George cried out. "Oh! Can you help?"

The lost property man rushed out from behind the desk to help. I slid over the counter and put the copied ruby in its place in the handle of the Malacca umbrella.

I slipped back over the counter and said to the lost property man, "Is everything okay?"

Begonia got back on her feet and apologised, saying she felt faint as she'd missed breakfast. The clerk said, "Miss, breakfast is the most important meal of the day, isn't it, sir?"

"It is," I said. "In fact, ladies, I'd be delighted to take you both to a late breakfast."

The clerk smiled and said, "Well said, sir. It's a pleasure to see a gentleman in this city. "

The girls smiled, looked at me and said, "That's a very kind offer, thank you very much."

We left the clerk smiling and waving goodbye and as we walked back upstairs.

I said, "I think we got away with that. Begonia, get lunch upstairs; George, you walk over to the Pier and take the next ferry. I'll slip on at the back and make sure you're not being followed. We'll meet up tonight at the office and go over what happened, okay?"

They both nodded. Begonia went upstairs and George left by the side door. I gave her five minutes and then hurried to the landing stage. The ferry to Woodside was just getting underway. I leapt aboard and got a right look from the deckhand, but I was on the ferry. I made my way to the top deck, checking for unlikely passengers. George stayed where she was for the return journey. Everything looked to be secure, but then I spotted our lady friend, on her own, waiting to board. But how had she known we'd be on the ferry?

As I walked past George, I told her she was being followed and to get off at the Pier Head and walk back to the office. She nodded. I kept well back from George as she left the ferry I and followed her and her lady friend back to the office. I didn't think anybody followed me, but after the episode in Calderstones, I wasn't sure. George opened the office and went inside. Our lady friend watched for a few minutes and then walked down the lane towards Victoria Street. I didn't follow, as no one else was walking in the lane.

Chapter 11—Laying the bait

George had the coffee on as I walked in.

George said, "Who followed me?"

"The woman again—she's smart and difficult to spot. I suspect they work in shifts. It's a mystery how they followed you onto the ferry. Better ring Begonia in a while and see if she noticed anything on her way back to the office?"

"Okay, to recap, boss—we've got a dummy ruby in place. The real one is with us, and we have another copy. They're following us, but they don't know where the ruby is and don't know where Jasmin is hiding out, correct?"

"Correct."

"So now, what's the plan?"

"I think Mr Daud needs to get kidnapped and taken to his bank where, amazingly, the ruby is in a safe deposit box!"

"Boss, do you think they will buy that?"

"It's the only way to separate the gangs. If they get the ruby, they may decamp to London and that just leaves one gang to deal with. They must know of the lost property office, and she knows you and Begonia so..."

"That hasn't worked out in our favour, boss. Maybe Begonia should stay with Binns and Jasmin. In fact, maybe they should all go to Binns's place in Wales?"

"That just leaves you and me here to sort out the gangs."

We sat there thinking it through. I rang Mr Daud and told him what had happened and my worries for the next part of our plan. He said he agreed it appeared to be a delicate situation, but he had complete faith in us. I thanked him and said I would ring him tomorrow morning.

Binns rang: "Eneko, I am sending a messenger round with some film that needs to be developed. All the gang members and cars they were using are on it."

"Binns, you are a godsend, mate. I'll get them done asap and ring you later. "

The messenger arrived, and I went downstairs to develop the film. I finished up and left the photos to dry and went upstairs to grab a coffee. Someone was in the office with George. I could hear voices; I stopped to listen.

"Okay sweetheart, you tell your boss that we want the item today or else, got it?"

"What if he asks me what the item is?"

"Don't play the fool with me. We'll be back at 6 pm."

I heard the door close with a bang. I went through to the office. "You okay, George?"

"Yeah, thinks he's a tough guy and so does the woman with him, a real bitch."

"They must really think we're a pushover to tell us what time they're coming to call. We need a meeting with Binns, pronto."

I rang Binns and told him what had just happened. He said he'd be round in an hour after making sure Mr Daud and Jasmin were safe. I told George to lock the office, and we went down to the basement. The photos were ready—George picked out the two who had come to the office, and I recognised the other one from the group. The other group of four I didn't recognise, neither did George.

I handed George the Beretta, and I took my Browning. The doorbell was ringing as we got back to the office. George opened the door and Binns slid through the door. "Two in a car up the road; the lady is looking at records in Rushworths."

I placed the photos on the table. Binns picked out the group of four and the car they were driving in. They all looked like the muscle.

"Not a brain between them," said Binns.

"Maybe it's her with the brains," said George.

"And no sign of the sisters, either! Okay, George, can you ring Sugar with the other number plate and tell him I'll send the photos round now with a cabbie? And get him to ring me later with names if he can, please?"

"Binns, this is going to be tricky. We can't really take them to pieces when they swan up at 6 pm!"

"No, Eneko, you're just going to listen to what they have to say and take it from there. I'll take a shufti now and let you know what they're up to. I'll be outside at 6 pm."

"Okay, Binns, see you later."

George put the photos in an envelope and called for a cab. I put on some coffee and grabbed some leftover tortilla from the fridge and cut up some bread. George lit up a couple of Passing Cloud. A knock on the office door brought George to life. She opened it and gave the cabbie the envelope and the address. She came back to the kitchen, sat down, and ate.

"Do we have a plan, boss?"

"No, let's just play it by ear. If they cut up rough, we're both armed."

George said, "I may get nervous."

"Let me do the talking and let's see where we go."

We sat around for the rest of the afternoon. George rang Begonia and said she'd meet her in the White star at 7 pm. She also rang Jasmin, and they had a long conversation with some laughs and giggles.

"She sounds cheerful?"

"Yeah, she is quite a character. She knows loads of people around Allerton. Evidently, that was where she used to go with her friends after school and on the weekends."

As soon as the phone rang, George answered: "Hi Sugar, yeah he's right here, hang on."

"Hiya mate, what's going on?"

"You don't do half measures, Eneko, do you? Nasty bunch all muscle except our lady friend. She's tied up with a real old legend. Do you want me to pay them a visit? Be my charming old self?"

"No, not for now, but I imagine we'll need you later. What happened down at the docks?"

"Not sure, but the word is drugs, so we'll see and take it from there. You take care, mate. "

"As always, Sugar."

George appeared to be a mite apprehensive. I smiled and kissed her on the forehead. The evening was still light and quite clear. The door opened with a bang and in came the two heavies, followed by the lady.

"We've come for the item," she said.

I looked her up and down. She was 40ish, bottle blonde, slim and well dressed.

I said, "My partner told me about your demands. I'm afraid you've out of luck."

"Really," she said, "I don't think so. If you don't supply us with the item, my boys will, I'm sure, be able to persuade you both."

The two pieces of muscle took out some knuckle dusters and came closer.

"Don't you think that's old-fashioned, threats, really?"

The bigger of the duo came at me. I sidestepped his attempted jaw breaking swing and kicked him in the knee and followed that with a blow to his temple—he didn't get up. The other one tried to kick me. I replied with a kick to the head and down he went. I turned and our lady friend had a gun pointing at me. "Enough of this comedy—give me the ruby, now."

Silence, then George said, "I'd put that gun down if I were you."

The lady turned to be confronted by a Beretta pointing straight at her.

"Do you know how to use that, dearie?"

"Try me."

The lady looked at me, shrugged and put the gun on the table. I picked it up, emptied it, and gave it back to her.

"Thanks for dropping in, but we're not buying today."

She glared at me, scowled at George, and said to her still moaning associates: "Get up and let's go."

"Ruby tomorrow, or things are going to get rough," she said, turning towards me.

She stormed out of the office, her two heavies staggered out after her. George looked very calm and controlled. "We should have shot them now because we're going to do it later."

"Think of the mess, George."

She smiled, "I'm up for a quick bath and then I'm off to meet Bee. Want to join us?"

"Yeah, why not?"

George got the bath going, and I waited for Binns. He came in and looked around. "Did it all go okay?"

"The two heavies tried their luck with some knuckle dusters and then madame produced a gun, but George did the same. But now they know what they're up against and forewarned, so it could all get very nasty."

George yelled something in Welsh, Binns replied, and George laughed. Binns said, "I'm going back home and I'm going to have a think about moving Jasmin and Mr Daud to Wales before all this kicks off. Call you in the morning. I wouldn't worry about the mob tonight. I heard them talking as they got in their car. You've got them worried, but they may bring in reinforcements. The other crew are still in the Adelphi, living it up!"

I shut the office. George was already in the bath. I washed and then climbed into the bath.

"You, okay?"

"Yes partner, I was nervous before it started, but okay when it began. You must show me that kick to the knee. It's so fast and puts them out of the game."

"I will, with pleasure. What are we going to do with Begonia?"

"I'm worried, too. I think it's best if they all go up to my place and Rabbit can show them where all the other hidey-holes are, they would find it very difficult to find them up there, especially as spring has arrived and the leaves and bushes will form a shield. The problem is, I don't think she'll want to go!"

"She'll have to go along with Jasmin and Mr Daud. I suggest Binn's place. He knows it like the back of his hand, and he's got Rabbit and other help. And let's be honest, he could keep an army at bay up there."

"True, so what do we do?"

"We could get ourselves caught by the second gang and hand over the umbrella and they just leave. But that will not work. Let's get organised, talk to Begonia at the pub and see what she has to say."

We had to take one gang out of the scenario to have the odds more in our favour, but how? What we didn't need is for them to join forces that could prove fatal. The more I thought about it, George, Binns, and I needed to be on hand to take care of things. Somehow, we had to get the rest to the safety of Wales.

I got dressed in cords and a roll-neck sweater. George looked great in a pair of denim pants from Paris and a sweater. We strolled down to the White Star. It was a pleasant evening with clear skies and warmth.

Chapter 12—Making it happen

The White Star was busy, but we found a table in the back room, and the barmaid came over to take our order.

"Evening sir, what would you like to drink?"

I looked up, expecting to see Maisy, but the barmaid was none other than Maisy's sister, Maggie. She looked a deal better than the last time I saw her. Her hair was its natural colour, light brown. She'd put on some weight and her eyes were clear and bright.

"Two G&T's please, Maggie."

She smiled and disappeared back to the bar, which Maisy was running.

"Who was that?"

"Maisy's sister, Maggie."

"Maisy told me about her and how you helped. You've done an ace job there, boss."

I nodded, Maggie came back with the drinks, I introduced George, she smiled, "Maisy has mentioned you, nice to meet you." Smiles all round before she was called away to another table. Begonia arrived with a G&T in her hand. "Evening gang, you all look relaxed, it must be the G&T's?"

Begonia sat down and gave us both a long look. "What are you two cooking up? I could hear brains whirring from the bar?"

George took the lead: Bee, you're going to have to disappear to Binns's place with Mr Daud and Jasmin for a while. "

"What the hell for?"

"Bee, it's just for a few days then I'll come up and join you, but first we have some nasty people to sort out, so please don't get upset."

"When?"

"Tomorrow afternoon, we have a plan all worked out. You and I will take the Underground to Hamilton Square, Binns will drive Jasmin and Mr Daud to Hamilton Square. You jump in with them, and he'll meet up with Rabbit nearby. Binns will make sure you're not being followed. I'll walk to Woodside and take the ferry and meet up with Binns as he comes back to Liverpool via the branch tunnel."

"Okay, what do I need to pack?"

"You can pack that Paella dish that Pedro gave you the other day."

Begonia laughed, "Nothing to say, Eneko, your new partner, sounds like she's in charge."

I swore at her in Basque. She laughed and blew me a kiss. George smiled, "Bloody foreigners."

"Okay, Begonia, so tomorrow morning, ring Pedro and tell him what's going on and then pack. You and George wait for me to leave tomorrow. They'll follow me and that should give you the chance to go to Central Station. I'll drop them and take the ferry to Woodside and make sure George is not being followed, and then we'll take it from there."

George raised her glass, took a swig, and said: "To the victor, the spoils."

We drank, and the girls kissed me and headed off home. I told George to be careful, and I'd see her first thing in the morning.

Back at the office, I put the coffee on and poured a large Remy. I needed to speak with Binns to give him enough time to get things ready and inform Rabbit. With a coffee and Remy at hand, I phoned Binns and ran him through what George had put on the table. He said that wasn't a problem, and he'd bring Rabbit up to speed. He reckoned the guests would be as safe there as anywhere as Rabbit had ex-paras to call on in time of need. I agreed that was a sound plan.

But George, Binns and I needed to get together tomorrow evening and draft a plan and get ready for trouble. We agreed to meet up after he picked up George the next day. After I put the phone down, I tried to work out where this was going. The sisters mustn't be as smart as I thought they were unless they were just biding their time and had let us do all the donkey work. I locked up and went to bed.

The phone woke me at 4 am. I answered and George said, "Eneko, someone is trying to break in but so far the door is holding."

"I'll be right there."

I grabbed some pants and a t-shirt, no time for a gun, so I picked up a Kendo stick and rushed out of the office. As I turned the corner, two of them saw me and came running—knuckle dusters glistening in the lamplight. I was in no mood for half measures. My Kendo stick did its business—I left them wailing in the road. Two more armed with knives came towards me. I heard George yell, "I'll take the short arse." The shorter one advanced on George as I attacked the other one. He wasn't expecting a Kendo stick as I winded him and then knocked him senseless. The shorter tried attacking with his knife, but George caught him with a fearsome roundhouse kick and knocked him out.

"I said get Begonia and come to my place. We've got weapons there if needed."

"Right boss."

We went past the bloodied bunch, who were trying to get to their feet and swearing like troopers. Begonia looked a little shaken, George looked very calm.

I said, "Girls, you sleep in my bedroom. I've got the couch." Begonia kissed me goodnight, and I hugged George, "You were terrific, now get some sleep."

I tried to sleep, but I kept waking, so I got up and made some coffee. The bedroom door opened, and George appeared. "I smelt the coffee."

We sat down, drank coffee, and smoked in silence. Finally, George finished her coffee and cigarette and broke the silence. "I think this is going to get a lot worse. That's both gangs well and truly humiliated. They will not take that lying down."

"That's given us an edge, George. It'll make them think hard, so in the meantime we must use it. Once we've got everyone in Wales, we go on the attack. I think they're bound to follow us, but we have a massive advantage there and one they know nothing about."

"They won't know what they're letting themselves in for in Wales. You're not just a pretty face, boss."

"Pretty face, eh?"

"Too pretty, even Rhian thinks so, but I like it like that, girly."

"Jesus! Enough of the compliments, thanks."

George grinned, kissed me, "Can I use the shower?"

"You know there's no need to ask. When you've done, we'll sort out the weapons."

George finished showering, and we crept past Begonia and into the basement. George took the beretta, loaded it and took a few extra magazines. I checked the Browning and then took out the Colt. George whistled, "I haven't seen that before!"

"No, I keep it for special occasions, and this is one of those times." Upstairs, Begonia was still sound asleep, not yet stirring from her slumber. George put the coffee on and made some toast.

"Morning, Bee, just in time for coffee and toast."

Begonia mumbled and sat down; eyes still half closed. "You look tired, Begonia."

She raised her face and said, "Blame her, she tires me out."

George kept pouring the coffee and buttering the toast. Binns called on the phone: "Let's get moving early. I want our party up and secure by the afternoon, so my spotters can see if anything untoward is happening. All my men have walkie-talkies, so communication is not a problem. And I have someone at the pub waiting for a call from us. Rabbit will be near Hamilton Square at 9:30 am, so see you later."

"Okay, we'll be there."

"Change of timing girls, same plan, but we're going earlier. I plan to leave here at 8:30 am. So, if you leave at 8:45 am, you should have plenty of time to get to Hamilton Square to meet Binns."

"Eneko, have I got time for a shower?"

"Not a problem.

"Do you girls need to get anything from the apartment?"

"I'll get the bags now, boss. Bee's travelling light this time, just three suitcases!"

Begonia smiled and then reminded me of how fluent her Basque was.

George warned her, "I'm getting Eneko to teach me Basque, then we'll see."

"Or we could both learn Welsh, I added."

If looks could kill, I went to make some more coffee and left Begonia in the shower.

After about 5 minutes, Begonia yelled, "Eneko, do you have a fresh towel, please?

"Yeah, hang on."

Begonia opened the door, and I handed her the towel. She turned around, and I noticed her bottom was a little red. She said: "It's your fault, you and that bloody book collection of yours."

George returned, bags at the ready. We had another coffee each, and we were all set to go. I gave George some travelling money, kissed them both. I grabbed my jacket and walked out into the morning air. A chill morning, but the mist would soon burn off. I strode along Dale Street, which was in the throes of the morning rush hour. A tram was moving off, so I jumped aboard and noticed two figures trying to keep up with me but failing. As we got towards Water Street, I hopped off so the pursuers could see me. I walked down towards James Street Station, bought a ticket and then, instead of going onto the platform, exited, and sidled down to the Pier Head.

The tide was going out, so I raced down to the Landing stage just as the Woodside Ferry was about to leave. On board I looked at passengers arriving late, but no one looked familiar. The ferry arrived at Woodside and the passengers disembarked. I went with them and took up a position that overlooked the ferry and the road coming from the train station. After about 15 minutes, George arrived and went to buy a ticket. She was being followed by one person: nobody I'd seen before. He stood, looked around, and tried to appear invisible. The passengers finally boarded; I was the last aboard. The ferry left, and a car screeched to a halt by the terminal. Three men leapt out, two of whom I recognised. They seemed to be at a loss. But they jumped back in their car with the man who had been following George. No doubt trying to beat the ferry by heading back through the tunnel to meet the ferry at the Pier Head. George went up to the top deck.

"Did you see them in the car? Do you think they'll beat us back to the Pier Head?

"They won't beat the ferry, boss. Let's hope they haven't left someone at the Pier Head."

"Yeah, there seem to be more of them coming out of the bloody woodwork."

We raced off the ferry, didn't notice anybody hanging around, and went onward towards the tunnel. Binns came sweeping around the corner, stopped, we jumped in and sped off. Binns did his usual anti-following technique by racing up and down back alleys and stopping and starting until he was sure we weren't being pursued. He shot up to the Philharmonic, parked in Hope Street, and said, "Let's get a drink and have a chat."

Chapter 13—A few beers

Binns found an unoccupied corner in the bar. The barman signalled he'd be over in a minute. From where we were sitting, we could see the front door just in case they had followed us.

George said, "Those bastards need taking down a peg or two. Do you think we got away with that? I need a drink to calm down."

Binns said: "For now, but I think we're living on borrowed time. Let's hope that Jasmin, Begonia, and Mr Daud are safe and sound with Rabbit and friends."

The barman caught my eye and raised the phone. I walked over, "Eneko speaking."

"Eneko it's me, Begonia."

She then lapsed into Basque and explained that a car had forced them off the road and they crashed into a telegraph pole. And they had forced Mr Daud and Jasmin into another car. Rabbit put up a fight, but they overpowered him and began hitting him with their pistols. A car stopped and a young guy jumped out and attacked them. He kicked the hell out of them and only stopped when they pointed a pistol at him. Then they pulled the injured guys into the car and drove off. Rabbit got hurt and our car is kaput, but the young man said he'll give us a lift.

"Okay, Begonia, put the young guy on the phone and I'll talk to him."

"I am grateful for your help, my friend. Is the car able to be driven?
"

"No, the front axle has gone, but I can get it towed right away. But your friend needs to go to the hospital, mate. He's pretty banged up?"

"I'll be there in twenty minutes. Can you grab a cab and get my mate and Begonia to the hospital, and I'll sort out any costs when I get there? Where are you?"

"We're at the Bottom of Argyle Street. I'll get things sorted with the cabbie and get your friends to the hospital."

I dropped the barman a fiver and went over to the table. Binns was already on his feet. "The proverbial has hit the fan. Let's get a move on."

On the way, I explained what had happened. Binns looked calm, but I felt he was seething. George looked at me, her eyes cold.

"I'll get the motor to a garage. Why don't you two head over to the hospital and see how Rabbit and Begonia are okay?"

"Okay, boss."

Binns had the motor zipping along, and we made it in 18 minutes. At the bottom end of Argyle Street, the Land Rover looked a little lopsided and was just about to be towed away. Binns went over and spoke to the driver and money changed hands and with a wave, the tow truck disappeared up the road. A young bloke got out of a Ford Zephyr. He cut quite a dash—a real Teddy Boy. He was lithe and lean and looked confident. Before I could say a word, George grabbed him and kissed him on the cheek, "Thanks for helping my friends, you're ace—I love your outfit."

He looked flummoxed, but smiled, anyway. "Your mates have gone to the accident and emergency at Arrowe Park Hospital. I thought it best to keep them away from around here."

"I'm Eneko, that's Binns, and she's George. We owe you one, mate."

"I'm Harry, but most people call me Tank."

Binns said, "We're off to the hospital, Eneko. I'll call you at your place later."

"Tank?"

"Yeah, I knew I'd get called up, so I joined the army as a mechanic, and they put me in the Royal Tank Regiment. I was always good with engines and mechanics, got it from my Uncle Brian, I suppose. I got posted to Korea, a tough spot, bloody nightmare in fact, but I survived and here I am."

He was in his early twenties, tallish, lean, and languid, but with a look of a coiled spring about him. He had a mop of black hair, piercing blue eyes, a straight nose, and a very enigmatic smile—I liked what I saw.

"Where do you live, Tank?"

"Just off Broadgreen Road."

"Your Uncle Brian wouldn't work with Ted Lenton, would he?"

"Uncle Ted! Yeah, do you know him?"

"I've known him since I was a kid. Can you give me a lift back and I can buy you a pint and have a chat?"

"Step into my car."

The Ford Zephyr looked in mint condition and the engine purred when Tank started it up.

We stopped off at the White Star and Tank got a few strange looks from some regulars. Maisy served us with a beaming smile, and she ushered into the back room, where we could talk without interruption.

"Begonia said you landed a couple of nice kicks before they pulled some guns."

"They were nasty bastards, killers, I reckon. Yeah, I did karate and kickboxing in Korea and have kept at it ever since, but only by myself. To be honest, I miss the action and esprit de corps of Korea in some ways, not the war, but just the feeling of excitement."

"I could do with another pair of eyes checking on things for me and your fighting skills could also come in handy paid, of course. I'm in the private investigation business. I'll explain it all when we have more time."

"Well, I don't know what to say, but yeah, I'm in."

We talked about Korea, fighting and driving and fixing tanks and, of course, Uncle Ted. Tank enjoyed working with his hands and was okay with his own company.

Begonia, George, and Binns interrupted our chat. Both Begonia and George gave Tank a big hug and sat on each side of him. Binns grabbed Tank by the hand.

"We owe you one lad that took courage facing down a loaded gun."

Tank said, "They were just punks. How's your mate?"

"He's complaining because they are keeping him in overnight, but he's hurting and they've had to stitch his head up, but I'm going to pick him up tomorrow. I spoke to the bloke from the garage, and he reckons the Land Rover will be ready in a couple of days. But we've got more serious stuff to get sorted, Eneko."

"All right, I reckon Tank is now part of the team, but we need to do some thinking. Let's head up to the office and get started."

We finished our drinks and headed up to the office. I showed Tank around and gave him a quick idea of what we did as a business and the state of our current job. Then Binns took over, and they started talking about the army, weapons, training, and arenas of combat. George put on the coffee and Begonia grabbed the Remy. I could see Binns was checking Tank out. And the girls seemed happy to be in his company.

Binns finally spoke up, "Okay, I'll pick Tank up tomorrow to see how Rabbit is faring and then we'll check out the Land Rover and get Rabbit back home, meanwhile you lot wait for the call from the scum that have got Mr Daud and Jasmin and then we'll get the wheels humming. See you later."

Begonia whistled, "Tank's a looker, eh! And what a fighter! You should see him in action. He moves like a ballet dancer and kicks like a mule."

"That's ace, someone else to train with apart from you, boss."

"I hope he can use a gun. I've got a feeling we're going to need all the weapons we can get our hands on. Okay, let's rustle up something to eat and then an early night. I'll sleep on the couch, so we all keep each other safe."

I didn't sleep well—I kept thinking about Mr Daud and Jasmin. Those bastards that were holding them had better go easy or there would be blood on the moon.

Chapter 14—-The Ransom

I looked at my watch: 7 am and the phone was making a din. As I picked it up, George and Begonia were standing right behind me. George grabbed a pen and some notepaper.

"Sora speaking."

"Listen pal, we want the ruby today or your friends go for a swim."

"How do you want to do the changeover?"

"Somewhere where I can see you coming from a long way, like Calderstones Park."

"Okay, what time?"

"Let's say 8 pm, it's getting dark by then, but I'll still be able to see you. Walk down to the bandstand and I'll meet you there. Bring the ruby and I'll have your friends ready."

"Did you get that, girls?"

"Yeah, we did. Bee is thinking what I'm thinking. What's the plan?"

"Well, they will not do us any favours. We need backup, somebody with a rifle back in the trees covering us. I wonder if Binns has one at his place here in Liverpool?"

George said, "Not sure, but I do. Binns brought it up from Wales weeks ago. It's all set to go, and I've got my original Bramit suppressor with it. It doesn't make a sound."

I started laughing, "George, you never, never cease to amaze me. That's part one covered—but you know they'll want to keep the upper hand. I imagine they'll drive and then walk across the meadow towards the bandstand. I'll front up, if you could get in that ditch that runs in front and take up a position there and be ready to fire."

"Okay boss, what's Bee going to do?"

"Stay here with Tank and keep an eye out for any unwanted visitors. The other crew could be on the move. Right, I'll get in touch with Binns, and he can relay the message to Tank. George, you get your weapon sorted out and Begonia, you get ready for work. Okay?"

I rang Binns and ran him through my plan. He agreed but suggested Rabbit stayed with Begonia in the office and Tank came with us. I agreed it seemed more sensible.

I left the girls to it and went downstairs and got myself organised. By the time I'd finished, Begonia had gone to work, and George came down with her sniper rifle. It looked the business, especially with the suppressor fitted. She loaded the rifle and lined it up and fired a few rounds, no sound, and all hits.

"Looking good, George, though it looks like it's got a kick."

"Not wrong boss, it takes a bit of getting used to."

George put it into a sports bag and said, "Okay, I'm ready for action."

We went back upstairs and got back to work, George to her typing, my contribution, coffee, and toast production. George suggested an amount for Tank—I nodded.

Lunchtime arrived, and so did Binns, Rabbit, and Tank. Rabbit looked like he was in pain but could still smile. George started talking to him in Welsh. I heard him say okay amongst the Welsh. George started making coffee and sandwiches. Binns grabbed me by the arm. "There's a carload of those idiots up the street. Any ideas?"

"No, not yet."

"Where's Begonia?"

"At work."

"They could have followed her, maybe, she should have taken the day off. She didn't answer the phone at the office when I rang. A lady answered and said Begonia had gone for lunch."

"George, where does Begonia go for lunch?"

"Bee goes to the Kardomah in Church Street; she gets on well with Ruby."

As I went to grab my jacket, Tank said, "You're busy. I'll check it out."

Binns said, "Eneko, if things go to plan this evening, I'll take Jasmin, Mr Daud, Rabbit, and Begonia to my place in the hills. There, we have a real advantage. When you get back, pick up the Land Rover that's being repaired, then we'll have two off-road vehicles."

George passed the coffees around and Rabbit got stuck into the sandwiches and a big fruit cake! Silence as we ate, interrupted by the phone ringing, I picked it up.

"En, Ruby from the Kardomah here. A massive scuffle just broke out, some scum bags began slapping Begonia around, so I picked up me broom but before I could start swinging. A young lad jumped in and gave the three of them a right battering. Chairs, tables, and coffee were all over the place. I've had to move the customers into the back and offer them coffee on the house."

"Ruby, you know I'll cover the cost, but what happened to Begonia?"

"She's fine, just a little shook up by those nasty bastards. The young lad said he's bringing her to your place."

"Thanks Ruby. Did the boys in blue arrive?"

"No scuffers yet, and by the time they do, it'll be as good as new. Another couple of villains dragged the scumbags out. I didn't see any trouble or recognise anyone. See you, En."

I put the phone down. All three of them were looking at me.

I said, "Begonia's okay, Tank to the rescue again! "

The office door opened, and Tank and Begonia came in. George rushed over to Begonia, and they disappeared into the bathroom.

Binns said, "Tank, you're growing on me, mate. Sounds like you had a bit of a workout?"

"Utter scum, they need a real sorting out. Two were outside, standing by a car. I heard the commotion and went into the cafe. I nobbled two of them: one's got a broken jaw; another has some dodgy ribs plus a black eye or two. They had knuckle dusters and the one with the broken jaw had a knife. The only way to stop them is to shoot them. You know, in Korea I shot people because they were in a different uniform. I bet they didn't differ from me: a kid from an ordinary family from an ordinary home. But these bastards are different, real evil bastards.

Rabbit said, "Dead right Tank, you're spot on."

I looked at Binns, he smiled, "Tank me old son, you're one of us. I don't suppose you might have any weapons hidden away?"

"Is the Pope Catholic?"

George stuck her head out of the bathroom and raised an eyebrow or two. I said, "How's Begonia doing?"

"Bee's fine, just pissed off she can't fight like you lot."

Begonia came out of the bathroom a little red eyed and a bit bruised around the side of her face. She went over to Tank and kissed him on both cheeks, and said, "Thank you, Tank."

Tank looked embarrassed, but smiled and said, "Don't mention it. I enjoyed coming to the rescue of a maiden in distress."

"You sound like you're going to be a busy man," laughed George.

We spent the rest of the afternoon planning our first line of attack, then our fallback positions. Binns was, as usual, the effervescent tactician; Tank put forward a few options, as did Rabbit, much to my surprise. George said where she would need to be to offer covering fire. Rabbit and Begonia would stay at the office. Rabbit had his old pistol that saw action in the war. After recovering Jasmin and Mr Daud, Rabbit would drive them, plus Begonia, to safety in Wales. Binns and Tank would follow them just in case some scumbags were on to them. Then Binns and Tank would return and sort out our vehicles.

As the afternoon ended, I was sure we were all having doubts, but nobody said anything. George and I left around 6 pm. Binns and Tank were leaving a little later and on the lookout for villains. We got to Calderstones and did a recce—Binn's style. The ditch didn't seem like a sound idea in the daylight. George said she needed to be higher for a better line of sight. And the Mansion House would give her a clear sight of the handover. The Mansion House was getting ready to close. It only stayed open at night later in the season. Our friends would come in off Menlove Avenue on the other side of the boating lake so they could see us and have a simple escape route. Binns arrived and George took him to one side and explained things. He waited until the place was closed and then went around the back, worked his magic on the locks, and George was in. We waited. Binns and Tank had walkie-talkies. Tank to be George's sighter. Binns disappeared into the undergrowth, and I sat down by the steps so I could see the boating lake. The evening air cooled and most of the kids and parents called it a day.

I saw the group as they got out of their car. I could see Jasmin and Mr Daud were with them. One of them came walking towards me. He stopped about 40 yards away and said, "Do you have the ruby?"

"Yes."

"Then pass it over."

"I'll pass it over when my friends are standing next to me."

"No chance. If you want them back, pass over the ruby."

I heard a bang, then the sound of hissing as air escaped from a tyre. One of them got out of the car and shouted over to the one standing in front of me, "They've shot the tyre."

I said, "Let's do the deal like we said, or my snipers will pick you off one by one."

He glared at me, waved his hand, and Jasmin and Mr Daud started walking towards me. As they reached me, I said, "Keep walking until you get to the Mansion House." Mr Daud nodded and kept walking. I saw Binns give me the sign, so I threw the silk bag with the ruby in it over to the main villain. "I hope you've got a spare tyre, pal."

He opened the bag, checked it and without a word stomped off back to the car. I walked back to the Mansion House, Binns was organising the Land Rover, Tank jumped in, and they were off. George came round the corner with a sports bag in hand. I looked at her, gave her a big hug, picked up her bag, and we headed off to my car. In the car, I said, "Great shot, did Binns call that?"

"No, it was Tank. He's done this before."

"Sure, looks like it, but now we've got to get organised because unless they're totally stupid, they'll discover the ruby is a fake in a heartbeat."

Chapter 15—Counting the cost

George sat in silence all the way back to the office, lost in her own private thoughts. My brain was ticking over as well, trying to make some sense out of this operation. At this stage, I wasn't sure who was in control, although having Jasmin, Mr Daud, and Begonia out of the way and tucked away in Wales made me feel less on edge. I parked up and George led the way, opened the office, put on the coffee, and opened the Remy. I sat down and George brought over the drinks.

"Boss, I think Jasmin's destination was always going to be Liverpool. I spoke to her, and she mentioned that Mr Daud is a very resourceful and meticulous planner. And that's why Jasmin went to school here. She has roots. She's a stranger in her own land, whereas the sisters are not. I think Mr Daud has played us for fools."

"George, I think you're right. I believe this whole charade is a way of getting Mr Daud back home, minus the sisters. His only mistake was not taking the sisters seriously. The set of clues was, of course, made up for Jasmin, as she alone would know which city they were talking about. The sisters, I think, got lucky and got some people together in London who are smart and on the ball. I'm sure they don't have any genuine interest in the sisters' plight, just the money, so they need to be kept close at hand; a real nasty bunch."

"What now?"

"Let's sleep on it. Binns and Tank will be here tomorrow, so we can decide what to do. But we must be careful, as those southern idiots could turn up any time. George, you spend the night here. There're loads of pyjamas in the cupboard along with extra towels and we've got our guns. What could go wrong?"

George smiled, kissed me on the cheek, and went into the apartment. I heard the shower then silence, "Goodnight, boss."

"Sweet dreams, George."

I showered, grabbed a couple of blankets, and made up the couch and dozed off. George woke me up whispering in my ear and pulling me into the bedroom and into bed where she wrapped herself around me, kissed me on the cheek and said goodnight. I fell asleep. No dreams, no nightmares, no sweats, just a wonderful feeling of wellbeing. The sound of bacon cooking and the smell of coffee woke me. When I got to the office, George passed me a cigarette and a fresh cup of coffee.

"Did you sleep well, boss?"

"Like a baby, thanks."

"Me too. I felt safe and warm."

She handed me a bacon sandwich. There was a knock on the front door. George opened the door and Binns and Tank came in.

"Coffee is ready, bacon sandwich. Anyone?"

Binns said, "No, we've already had breakfast, but the coffee sounds good."

George said, "How's the mountain hideout?"

"Perfect. Everybody has settled in, even Begonia. Rabbit has rigged up some booby traps, so they are safe and sound. And I've got some more news. Binns put a set of keys on the table."

"What's that, Binn's keys to the pile in Wales?"

"No, George, a place much closer to home. I'll show you around after we've finished coffee."

George looked at me, eyebrows raised. I said, "Give me 5 minutes to get dressed."

I grabbed some clothes, and we headed out of the door, Binns pointed up the lane, we followed, we got to the top and we turned into Temple Street, walked along for about 50 yards, and stopped outside a warehouse that was busy, with lorries taking in wood and other supplies. Binns stopped near the end of the building in front of a steel door, opened it, and we entered a hallway with just another steel door in front of us. Binns used another key, and the door opened to reveal a lift. We entered the lift. Binns pressed the button, and we rose.

After a brief journey, the lift stopped, the door opened, and we entered an apartment. The place was enormous, with windows that were the entire height of the walls. The place ran the length of the building. We checked it out. It had everything, including 4 bedrooms, each with its own bathroom. We looked at each other and just laughed. The place was a palace with solid wooden floors, teak by the look of it, amazing stonework and brickwork. The give-away was the furniture-oriental with lots of malacca ware.

"Is this Mr Daud's weekend place, Binns?"

"Yes, this is where he stays when he's in Liverpool. He owns the whole place, lock, stock, and barrel. All the merchandise is from his part of the world, and it's then sold on to wholesalers nationwide. This is his present to Jasmin, and he wants you, Eneko, to get Begonia and Mr Bengoa to run the operation for him when he returns home."

I was stuck for words, but not for long. "So, this plan of Mr Daud's is to get Jasmin safe and sound here in Liverpool after we sort out the villains?"

Tank said, "That's about it, Eneko. We reckon we should allow the villains with the ruby to track us to Wales, sort them out and then come back and take on the other mob."

"Sounds like a plan, so we'll let them follow George and I while you and Tank go on ahead and set the trap."

"Don't get stopped, and we'll have you covered as soon as you get past the village. Tank and I will leave from here. The other Land Rover is fixed, so we're on the road. See you up there. Any problems ring the pub, they'll get a message to me."

George said, "Take care boys," and kissed them both. Binns murmured something in Welsh, and she smiled.

George and I left the warehouse and scooted back to the office. I told George to pack while I went and got the Land Rover from the coopers's yard. Frank was watching his friendly urchins playing football. I chatted for a while and mentioned that I was going away for a few days and asked him to keep a lookout on my office. If anything happens, just call the police. The Land Rover looked spick and span. I raised my eyebrows. Frank pointed to the boys. I gave the kids half a crown each, and they looked well pleased.

One of them said, "Is George going with you?"

I said "Yes."

"We'll look out for you. Can you give George a kiss for me?"

Frank laughed, "Cheeky little bugger, that's Eric. George is teaching him to read. She lends him comics and stuff. I reckon he's in love."

I smiled and drove off. I parked up and George and I made a big play of getting ready to depart. We went armed for hunting: sniper rifle, the three pistols and enough ammo for a war. I mentioned George's admirer. She laughed. "He's a little tinker, but he's bright. He'll be alright."

Chapter 16—Sharpshooters

We headed for the tunnel. I spotted two cars on our tail as we entered the tunnel. Our lady friend was in the front seat next to the driver. George was watching out for any other cars full of our friends. We left the tunnel and took the route to Wales on the A550. The two cars were still with us when a red Ford Zephyr cut in front of our trusty followers and forced them to miss the turning. A cacophony of horns followed that soon dissipated as we sped up along the road. The Zephyr blasted past and with a wave Tank was gone.

"He's a genuine character, Boss. A bit of luck with him coming onboard, I reckon."

"You're not wrong, George. I think Binns has taken him under his wings. He learns fast, bright as a shiny new button."

We drove on. After a while I spotted the same car following us, but at a distance. I drove at speed, but they kept up with no problem. As we came to Bylchau, I shifted gear and shot up the dirt track, leaving lots of dust flying in the air. I knew they'd spot that with no difficulty. The track was easier now that I could see where I was going. After about 15 minutes, we came to the junction. I raced up the steep track to the left and kept going. As we got nearer the cottage, Rabbit waved to us as we parked at the back of the property. Binns and Tank came out of the cottage.

I went over, "Everything okay, Binns?"

"Yeah, I've got two spotters further down with walkie-talkies, so we'll know when they decide to come up the hill. Mr Daud and Jasmin are inside with Begonia."

George swept past and nipped into the cottage to say hello and see how everyone was bearing up under the strain.

Binns said, "Rabbit is staying here in the yard with his shotgun. Tank is inside with a couple of pistols, us three are going to get set up over there above the road. Eneko, you stay here on the side of the road so you can see everything and use the walkie-talkie to keep in touch. George and I will set up one on each side to get them in a crossfire."

I went to ground and using the binoculars Binns had given me, I checked out the bottom part of the track. Their car came up, stopped and four got out, all armed.

I spoke over the walkie-talkie, "Binns, I've got four of them in sight walking up the track, but I'm sure they have another car with them."

"Yeah, I know the other spotters have reported in. There are three of them, but they're waiting in the car. George and I will shoot the tires out of the car that you've spotted. It may get them to move on, although I doubt it."

I heard a slight coughing sound and the tyres on the car went down with a bang. The woman made herself known and fired her pistol up towards us, not a hope of hell of hitting anything. A couple more coughs and the headlights went bang. I could see the gang was getting worried. They couldn't see us, but we could see them. She started giving them orders, and they spread out and took cover.

Binns and George started laying down a show of marksmanship, bits of trees and branches flying all over the place. The gang looked like they had had enough.

Their erstwhile leader yelled, "We know where you are, we'll come back with more men and sort you out, you bastards." Another cough and she hit the ground, hit in the shoulder by the look of it.

I called down, "Pick her up and don't come back. You've got 5 minutes, then we shoot."

"Okay, okay," someone shouted and two of them picked their leader up and half carried her.

Binns yelled down, "You can bring the other car up for her, but then beat it."

The other car came up the hill and somehow, they all got in and drove off.

Binns and George appeared, waved, and we all started back uphill towards the cottage. The walkie-talkie started crackling, Binns started waving, telling me to get a move on. At the cottage, Binns said, "The spotters have got 5 more coming up around the back of the cottage. You stay inside with Rabbit and look after everyone. Tank, George, and I will put the cat amongst the pigeons with the amount of fire we can put down the valley and don't worry, our spotters are armed as well, so they won't know what the hell hit them."

Tank came out of the cottage with a sniper rifle. George waved and the three of them started moving downhill. I went inside. Rabbit was by the side window that offered a view of the back of the cottage. Mr Daud, Jasmin, and Begonia were sitting down at the table, trying not to look concerned. I kissed Begonia on the cheek, shook Mr Daud by the hand, and hugged Jasmin. She looked at me, "Are we going to be alright, Eneko?"

"It won't be long now, just be calm and listen to Rabbit."

Rabbit let me out of the door, and I positioned myself behind a large oak tree and waited. The last line of defence. I heard the cough, cough of sniper rifles and yells and curses of men under extreme duress. Then silence. I thought it was all over when a shotgun came into view being held by one of the villains. I shot him in the shoulder, the shotgun went flying. He was on his back, looking at me. Next thing Tank arrived, nodded, and sent a message on his walkie talkie. He got the injured villain to his feet and began marching him down the hill. George came flying up the hill, took one look at Tank, who nodded in my direction, and ran over to me and hugged me. "You okay boss?"

"Yeah, that must have been their last chance, their bona fide hitman. It's all good. Rabbit is holding the fort. What's happening down the hill?"

"Four of them with wounds. Binns and I supplied the covering fire. Tank picked them off, all leg wounds. I don't think they'll be coming back."

We waited, then after about 10 minutes, we heard the car engine start up and move away. We saw Tank and Binns coming up the hill, smiling.

Binns said, "Great job lads and lass, they won't be coming back, and our spotters are making themselves obvious by following them. And they'll get rid of the damaged vehicles. You did well there, Eneko. I didn't see that villain making it to the top."

"Belt and braces approach, never think it's over until it's over."

Binns got on the walkie talkie and when we got to the cottage, Rabbit and all were there to meet us, hugs all round, even from Mr Daud!

The girls got the coffee going with some bara brith to go with it and, of course, a shot of Remy. We took it in turns to keep lookout. Nothing, just the sound of country life. I heard the walkie talkie crackle into life, and Binns saying something in Welsh and silence.

Binns said, "The bad lads have long gone, but to be on the safe side we've got lads spotting on all roads, so it's time to relax."

Everybody started talking at once. Jasmin seemed to stay close to Tank. George caught my eye and winked. Begonia was holding onto George and laughing and crying at the same time. Mr Daud looked serene. Binns caught my eye and he and Rabbit walked outside.

Rabbit spoke, "Eneko, just to let you know the locals think you've done us a massive favour and you have. We won't let you or ourselves down. This is a great time to start things going and build up the community."

"If it helps, that'll be great. This area deserves to be successful, and I'm sure you're the man to get it going."

Rabbit shook my hand and slapped me on the back, and left Binns and me to our thoughts. "Eneko, I saw tears in his eyes, mate. You've got a friend for life."

"Binns, these idiots won't stop, you know."

"Yeah, you're right, but they know they're going to need an army of shooters to take us. Is it worth their while?"

"Binns, I've been thinking about it. The villains want money, not rubies but cash. They know if they want to get us, it's going to cost them, dear, so why bother? They have two valuable assets, the sisters. Why not ransom them? Their country or sultanate is rich. Wouldn't they pay to get them back?"

"Yeah, Mr Daud says they are not popular. In fact, he said the people hated them."

"Yeah, but do the gangs know that? I think this is a plan by our Mr Daud to get rid of the sisters and for him to help run the country."

"But what about Jasmin? She's just like his daughter, remember?"

"Yeah Binns, I know. Mr Daud was following his boss's plan. That's why she went to school in Liverpool, that's why he's got that warehouse and that's why she studied medicine. He wants her to live in Liverpool and enjoy the freedom of this country. Women have little rights in Borneo!"

"Eneko, that's complicated. I'll leave the thinking to you. Let's get back inside. My brain is whirring."

Chapter 17—Dancing on thin ice

Inside the cottage, the mood was triumphant.

Jasmin said, "Why don't we go out and celebrate?"

"Rabbit said, "We've got the Jive dancing contest at the pub tonight."

Begonia, "Dancing? What a brilliant idea. I love dancing."

George looked at me. "It'll be fun. We can just stand at the back and watch."

Everybody got ready, and we all got into the vehicles that were at the cottage or just further down the road. I walked down with George and Begonia. The spring sunshine brightened everything; the sky was cloudless—with wildflowers searching for the sun.

I drove to the pub along the same road where a few hours ago gun fire was raining down on this part of the hill. George appeared pensive, maybe going through the action in her head. Begonia looked like she was getting ready for a night out. At the pub, people were entering their names for the competition. Jasmin and Tank were a couple, so were George and Begonia. This should be fun, I thought. Some young lads came in and one of them spotted Jasmin and made a remark that his mate thought was funny. Tank was having none of it and went over to them.

"That remark about that young lady wasn't funny, mate. You owe her an apology and fast before I lose my temper."

The lad looked like he was about to say something when a young woman grabbed him by the balls and spoke in Welsh. George grabbed my arm and said, "It's okay, just leave them to it."

The lad went crimson, but he walked over to Jasmin and apologised. Jasmin smiled and said, "I hope you can dance better than you tell jokes." And kissed him on the cheek. That brought the house down, lots of laughter and backslapping, people ordering drinks. The young lad went over to Tank and put his hand out and said something. Tank took his hand and slapped him on the shoulder.

George passed me a beer. I said, "What did the young lass say?"

"It doesn't translate that well into English, but she mentioned his balls were missing. He's called Owen, and that was his elder sister, Erin. She's brought him up, dad killed in the war and mum running the farm. So, she doesn't take any shit from her little brother. He just thought he was being smart. He's lucky Tank didn't thump him."

The party looked about to get going. A young fellah at the mic said it's time to get dancing and on came an American number and everyone started jiving.

Jasmin and Tank cut a real dash, and they looked terrific. Begonia grabbed a young man by the bar. The lad looked delighted to have a Spanish beauty as his partner. George and I went to the bar with Binns and Rabbit. Twenty couples were kicking up their heels. It was turning out to be quite a night. And every time the music stopped, they had to change partners; the idea being at the end of the night, the judges chose the best male and female dancer. Binns and I collared Mr Daud, and we went outside for a drink and a chat.

Mr Daud looked at me with an embarrassed look in his eye, "Eneko, I must apologise for my deviousness, but I had to make sure of Jasmin's safety—safe from her sisters and all the ramifications of power at home. As you have no doubt guessed, my Master's plan was always to have Jasmin in Liverpool. He knew he didn't have long for this world and concocted this silly scheme, but it has worked out, except for all the violence. I will return to my homeland and become part of a new government, run on democratic lines. I fervently hope that the sisters stay in Europe. They were both educated by a French governess, so they speak fluent French and have visited France many times over the years, and they know the country well. If they accept my offer, on behalf of the government, they will get a generous stipend to live."

"There's just one fly in the ointment, Mr Daud. Those villains from London are going to be out of pocket and extremely angry. They may well do something and use the sisters as an asset and demand a ransom from your government. Do you have any idea where they are at present?"

"I think they are in Cheshire somewhere, but I'm not sure. Do you think the gangsters will turn on them?"

"Do the sisters have unlimited funds?"

"No, but again, I'm not sure how much they have or have spent."

"Okay, let's get back inside and enjoy ourselves. The next step is up to the gangs, and they are way down on manpower."

The pub was lively when we stepped back in. Rabbit and Binns were laughing and pointing at Tank, who looked like he knew what he was doing. Begonia was all hair and swirling skirts, just like some of the young local girls. The man at the mic called time and said, "Right, it's a dance off between Jasmin and Tank and Begonia and Owen, so take your partners, please."

They took off and I must admit they were all superb. How they were going to choose a winner I did not know. After about 4 mins, the man at the mic called out, "Change partners for the last time, please."

Owen and Jasmin were looking great, quicker than Begonia and Tank. The music stopped. They counted the judges' papers: The man at the mic said, "The winners are Owen and Jasmin." There were cheers all round as the winners accepted their trophies and even more cheers when Binns announced drinks on the house courtesy of Mr Daud, who bowed.

Tank was chatting to Owen and Erin came over and grabbed Tank and took him on to the dance floor, and another young lad came over and asked Jasmin for a dance followed by another young lad who asked Begonia. The music blared out, and they were off and running. George laughed, "Tank will not get any rest tonight. The girls think he's gorgeous, and the same goes for Bee and Jasmin."

I looked at the party and thought this could be the lull before the storm, but I kept that to myself. I watched George. She was thrilled at the way Begonia was enjoying herself. I joined Rabbit, Binns, and Mr Daud at the bar. Finally, the frenetic music stopped, and some slow dance songs came on. Romance time! Jasmin pulled Tank back out onto the floor, followed by Begonia and George, and the rest of the dancers. Mr Daud caught my eye. "I think Jasmin likes Tank. They look good together, don't you agree?"

I nodded. He smiled. He looked surprised when a middle-aged lady asked him for a dance. I thought he would refuse, but he bowed and said, "Delighted, my dear!"

The evening ended, and we departed. Binns, Tank, Jasmin, and Mr Daud went up to his place, and I drove up to George's cottage. When we got there, the lights were on, and we could hear music. I climbed out, ready for anything, but George caught my arm. The door opened and Rhian was standing there.

"Come in, the coffee and Remy is ready." She kissed me and we went indoors. We sat around and George told her the story of the night with Begonia showing her new jive moves. George said, "That's me goodnight." She and Begonia went off to bed.

Rhian caught my hand. "Sorry about the other weekend. Come on, the bed's made up." We slipped into bed. It felt like it had been a long time.

Chapter 18—The new Landlord

I awoke to see three naked lasses, Rhian examining various parts of Begonia and George and muttering at how well the cuts and bruises had healed. "The sea and sun helped," she said. They turned and looked at me. "The perfect start to the day," I said. They attacked me, pulled the blankets from me and looked at my pale, white body.

"Apart from needing some sunshine, you need a shower," said George. I nipped into the bathroom before they bathed me. When I'd finished, I came out to the aroma of brewed coffee and bacon. God! It smelled good.

Rhian said, "I must go to work Eneko, I'm flat out now. Rabbit has told me all about the plans for the land. It is a superb idea, and I think it'll work. I know everyone is very excited — you'll no doubt be called Squire with all its privileges! But remember, I can shear anything without a sound." She jumped up, wrapped her legs around me, and chewed my bottom lip.

"How long can you keep me up here? I wonder. Let's find out soon." And she was gone.

Begonia came out from the bathroom with no clothes on and wandered back to the bedroom. I heard some giggles, so I put my boots on and wandered out to eat my breakfast in the morning sunshine. A glorious morning. The trees were getting greener by the day. I could see all kinds of birds chirping away and searching for food. The view down the valley was breath-taking. Spring brought out the best in this part of the world. I stood up and looked over to the other side of the valley and I imagined what it would be like to have sheep, cows, pigs, maybe even a horse or two wandering around the woods. Right now, nothing stirred. It would take a lot of work to get things right, but well worth it. I felt good, content to be helping to aid the local economy in finding its feet. Lost in my thoughts, I didn't hear George come out and refill my coffee cup.

"Beautiful, isn't it?"

I said, "It is, you know, I was just imagining what it would be like with animals all over the place."

"It'll be wonderful, with animals on the hills and in the woods. It helps nurture everything, wild herbs, mushrooms. You'd be staggered by how it'll change the entire landscape. Come on, we've got time. I'll show you around."

Begonia declined the offer of traipsing around hills. She said she was knackered from last night's exertions. She yelled that she'd make something to eat at about 3 pm. George led the way. We skirted the hill at the back of her property and wandered downhill into a stream that formed the border of the property. George explained that everything on this side was now mine. We climbed up the hill, which was populated with various evergreen and deciduous trees. George knew them all and pointed out oak, ash, beech, sycamore, birch, and cherry. And the various herbs, wildflowers, and mushrooms. She explained which trees and plants attracted which animals and birds. She said that with the different animals we'd introduce, that would improve the land and wildlife, a win-win situation. We clambered up to the top of the hill and George pointed out where the property ended. Miles bigger than I'd imagined. She said the animals would love it up here in the spring, autumn, and summer, plenty to eat and drink and shade when it got hot. George strode on and we meandered on a track for about 20 minutes until we came out by a barn. George went round the front and stopped. There stood a charming little cottage. I didn't know what to say.

"Lovely isn't boss. This and the barn would be a great place to live in or rent it out after you do it up a bit."

"No George, this is going to be my hideaway, close enough to nip round to your place for a coffee. You're right, the other cottage and barns we could do up and they could become part of the soon to be thriving cottage industry."

George laughed, "All you need to do now is learn Welsh. Don't worry, Rabbit and Binns know what they're doing, and the locals admire and trust them. In a couple of years, you won't recognise the place. Come on, I could eat a horse."

We walked back and I still couldn't get over the thrill, my piece of Welsh countryside. As we neared George's place, the smell of olive oil, fresh rosemary, garlic, and lamb roasting hung in the air. Binns and Tank were already drinking beer and turning the meat on the barbecue.

Binns waved. "Surveying the property, Eneko?"

"Yeah, George has just given the guided tour. It's much bigger than I expected and looks like a lot of work to me."

"You let us worry about that. It'll take time, but Rabbit knows what he's doing, and he's got top people and families working with him."

George went into the cottage and came out with plates and bread. Begonia came out armed with a tortilla and a tomato salad.

"Tank, I'm still knackered from last night. My legs don't want to move. How are you?"

"Yeah, the legs are complaining a bit, and Jasmin was still out cold when we left, and Mr Daud was reading a newspaper."

I said, "Let's tuck in because after we've finished, I'm off back to my place to make sure everything is okay, and I'll catch up with you three sometime tomorrow."

We ate and tried to plan but, in the end, we gave up. After lunch, we tidied up, packed the Land Rover, and headed back to Liverpool. George was in the driving seat, so Tank and Begonia were in the back and talked about dancing for most of the way back. I tried to keep calm, but I was alert and kept looking for problems. When we arrived back at the office, I said I'd give Tank a lift, but he said he'd borrowed Jasmin's key and was going to stay there. Mr Daud wanted him to check on the place and make sure the business was in good shape. So, we said we'd see him in the morning, and we filed into the office.

George said, "I'm going to run a bath. I'm tired and grubby."

Begonia yelled, "Me too."

George said, "You too, boss, your best plans seem to happen in the bath."

We all got washed up and entered the hot tub. It felt fantastic. We sat there with our own thoughts until Begonia said, "I think Jasmin fancies Tank and I know Tank fancies Jasmin. They spent last night together."

"They make a great couple, Bee. Mr Daud has asked him to sort out the business side of the warehouse. He wouldn't do that unless he trusted Tank. Mr Daud is a clever man."

I said, "I still think these villains are going to finish what they started. They want the money and if the sisters don't come up with the full amount, I reckon they are going to be in trouble. The ruby copy idea is dead, so they either come for us or, like I said, ransom the sisters."

"But would Mr Daud pay the ransom?"

"I think so, Begonia. That would be a successful outcome for Mr Daud. Jasmin is safe here, working as a doctor. She has friends. We know his plans and with the sisters out of the way, things should return to normal. If they kidnap the sisters, that will get them out of our hair and into Sugar's. He'd love it. I'll bring him up to speed tomorrow."

I got out of the bath first, got dressed and made some coffee and poured the Remy. The girls came in with those big woolly bathrobes and sat down and we half watched some tv for a while. The girls hit the hay in my double bed, so I slept on the couch.

Chapter 19—Tank to the rescue

The phone woke me. I answered, "Sora speaking."

"It's Tank, Eneko. Some lowlifes are checking the warehouse out and chatting to the lads, but they're not saying anything."

"Okay, watch them. I'll get dressed and come over. Are you armed?"

"Yeah, I'm still carrying. See you soon."

I got dressed and put the coffee on. George said, "Make enough for three."

By the time the coffee was ready, George and Begonia had their work clothes on. George fired up the Passing Cloud and waited for me to say something. "That was Tank, there are suspicious characters checking the warehouse out, but the staff are saying nothing. I'm going to nip over and see if I can find out anything. I'll be back before Begonia leaves for work."

The phone rang again. "Eneko, get a move on. They are about to leave in a minute. We should follow them."

"Hang on, I'll be two minutes. George, we're just going to follow the villains."

"Okay, boss."

I grabbed the Land Rover from the coopers's yard. Frank was already working. Little Eric yelled, "Is George in?"

"Yes, she's in."

I drove up the lane towards the warehouse. Tank was already outside waving for me to get a move on. He jumped in, "Left at the top."

We turned left and moved on to Dale Street. "That's them in the black Buick."

"Nice and inconspicuous, eh!"

"Makes it easier for us, Eneko. Just hang back a bit. We're not likely to lose them."

Tank was right. I kept vehicles in front of us as they made their way along the dock road with the Overhead railway clunking above us. The dock road near Bootle was still a mess from the blitz. They appeared to be heading in that direction but then turned and headed towards Crosby. We had no trouble following them, as the traffic was slow. After Crosby, they took the A59 towards Southport. We stayed well back as there was little traffic on the road. We lost sight of them as a lorry got in behind us. As we passed the turning for Formby, Tank signalled that they'd taken the Formby Road. I drove on until I could turn and then came back to the Formby turn off. We drove along. We were heading to the beach road when Tank signalled for me to stop.

"I think we need to go on foot from here, Eneko. In fact, you stay put ready to make a move and I'll do a recce and see if I can see what they're up to."

"Okay, I'll swing the Land Rover around and wait here."

Tank disappeared and was gone for a good 20 minutes. I was getting worried, so I opened the door and stepped out to a pistol barrel, pointing at my face. "Start walking," was the command. I did what I was told and started walking when I heard a crunch behind me. I turned to see Tank standing over the villain. "He's going to have a headache," said Tank. "Let's go!"

We jumped into the Land Rover and headed back out to the Southport Road. Tank kept looking out of the back window and, after about 5 minutes, he said, "Nothing following us. They haven't noticed he's missing yet. There were 6 or 7 of them all armed to the teeth and they're waiting for orders from somebody called—G—who I think is female."

"I'll stop at the nearest phone box, and we'll make some calls." Tank called Binns, and I called George and put her in the picture. Then I rang Sugar. He was in and was all ears as I explained what I'd seen in Formby. I mentioned they may disappear. He said he'd call the office when he knew what was going on. Tank took the wheel, and I tried to think things through.

Mr Daud and Jasmin are safe in Wales; George at the office, Begonia at work; Binns on his way to the office; Gunmen still in Formby; Sugar on the case. Where was the other gang? And where were the sisters?

All so very simple. Tank drove us back to Frank's. He waved, and we walked back to the office. Binns was already there, and so was little Eric.

"Hiya Boss," said Eric, "Do you need your Land Rover washed?"

"Great idea, young Eric."

I threw him the keys. He caught them and blew a kiss to George and scarpered.

George smiled, "He's a right case, but bright, his reading and writing are coming on like a house on fire."

"That's cos he's got a wonderful teacher," laughed Tank. "And he fancies you, too."

Tank ran everyone through what had happened at Formby, and I added the bit about getting held at gunpoint.

Binns said, "Okay, from now on, everyone carries a weapon. If we get stopped by the rozzers, we take our chances. We need to decide what to do with the sisters. We either warn them off and put them on the boat to France or something more drastic. These idiots from London need sorting out, but how and where? I think the gang we tangled with in Wales has left the scene. They were too shot up to want to hang around and get more of the same without seeing some big reward!"

The phone rang, George picked it up, "It's Sugar," she passed me the phone. I listened carefully, "Okay thanks mate, talk soon."

"Nothing there in Formby just signs of a quick exit and the Buick has gone, but that should be easy to trace. Sugar sounds interested, so he'll get busy."

The phone rang again. George picked it up. "Hi Bee, what? Are you sure? Okay, I'll ring you straight back. Bee just had two oriental looking ladies in the office, who spoke French and were delighted that Bee also spoke French. They said they were working for a shipping consortium and were looking for somewhere to store freight in transit and someone had mentioned the warehouse on Temple Street. Bee said she'd investigate it and get back to them. They're staying at the Adelphi under the name of Jannah and Mira Delacroix."

"Okay, now we're getting somewhere. Let's get Begonia to set up a visit at the warehouse as soon as possible. George, give Begona a ring and thank her for her quick thinking."

"Okay, boss."

"Ideas lads?"

Tank went first, "Well, they don't know about the top floor being an apartment. They know it's a warehouse, so they suspect something—maybe they think the ruby is stored there?"

Binns said, "Could be. They know Jasmin and Mr Daud are out of the picture in Wales, so unless they're looking for the ruby, what are they here for? Could be they're under increasing pressure from the gangs to come good with some real money?"

"I think it's time to check with Mr Daud about what money the sisters can lay their hands on and where? Binns, can you get word to Rabbit and maybe we can have a chat with Mr Daud and Jasmin sometime this evening?"

George was on the phone with Begonia. She replaced the receiver. "Bee is going to meet the sisters tomorrow morning at 10 am to show them around."

Tank said, "I'll stay the night again and be ready in the morning in case I'm needed."

"Good idea, Tank," said Binns. "I'll be around as well. In fact, I could stay overnight. Let's get round and have a chat with the lads who are working there and see if anything comes up."

"Okay lads," I said, "see you later. Call me if anything comes to light."

Chapter 20—Redefining the boundaries

George made coffee while I gathered my thoughts and wondered what I could get out of Mr Daud over the telephone this evening. George brought the coffee over and said, "Boss, can we talk?"

"Of course. What's up?"

"Little Eric, his family is struggling. Did you know he has a twin sister called Helen and they live with their mother, Viv, in a one room dump over the way? Viv is only 21 and works as a cleaner. The so-called father disappeared, but I think he comes around to get money out of her. It's unbelievable. Helen goes to school and is doing well and Eric, well..."

"So, how can we help?"

"It's a difficult one, boss. Viv is bright but broke and with no family. Her father died in the war; her mother in the Blitz, so her only relative is her grandfather, and he's not in the best of health. And Frank, of course, who dotes on her."

"Hang on George, you mean Viv was 13 or 14 when she had the twins?"

"Yeah, that's one problem and you know Eric's. But I've got an idea. Don't get mad though, it's just an idea, okay? I train Viv up to be the secretary. We put them in the apartment next to mine and Eric goes to school. He'll listen to you, boss. That'll free me up to be more of a business partner, and I'm sure Viv will be a wonderful addition to the firm. She's also pretty. When she's smartened up, she'll be a real asset to the firm. "

"Wow, George, you've given this a lot of thought. I'm impressed. Okay, you do the interview. I'll get Frank and some of his lads to make sure the apartment is in working order, and we'll take it from there."

"George came over, kissed me on the nose, "You're a lovely man, boss. "

"Just one thing, George. If Viv calls me boss, what are you going to call me?"

"En, of course, silly question."

I laughed, "Right, I'm just popping out to see Frank. Be back in twenty minutes."

Frank beamed his glorious smile when he found Eric's mum and his twin sister were going to move into the apartment. He'd get some lads to sort out the apartment starting tomorrow.

"Eneko, while you're here, I've got a pin with your name on it." He produced an oak barrel, pin size, for brandy that was copper bound and had my father and mother's name on it.

I didn't know what to say, so I just hugged him, and he ruffled my hair.

"Make sure you put only the best in that barrel, Eneko.

"You know I will, Frank."

George gave me a quizzical look when I got back to the office and grinned when I showed her the brandy barrel.

"That's what I call a barrel. Old Frank knows his onions."

George shot off to see Viv and the twins, and I waited by the phone. George was back by 6 pm with a very contented smile on her face.

"Vee is so happy and guess what, she can type. She did it at school. The bright young ones who could read, write and spell got trained up to be secretaries as part of the war effort. I haven't mentioned the flat yet. I thought I'd leave that to you."

"George, it's your decision. You manage it and I'll back you all the way, okay?"

"Okay En."

"I think tomorrow could be a big day. I'm expecting a call from Mr Daud tonight to see if we can iron out the details of how to finish this before the shooting starts. And make sure you take Viv to see Lavinia and sort her out with the works and make sure the twins have school uniforms and..."

"En, I've got it, okay. It's all under control. Vee is coming in on Monday as she needs to finish her cleaning job this week, but then she'll start. And seeing as it's Friday I'll put the bath on, Bee should be back any time now. Then we can settle down and have a few drinks. Bee is bringing the food."

While George was sorting out the bath, I laid out some clean clothes, just casual stuff, and grabbed some towels. The phone rang.

Binns said, "Eneko, we've had a chat with the gaffer who runs the warehouse. He seems sound and took a liking to Tank, as Tank has promised to get him a new transport manager, which is something they need. He has already met Mr Bengoa and thinks he's a proper gent, so we're looking good. Those idiots came round alright and wanted to know if they had any stuff from Borneo, so the gaffer showed him the Teak, Malacca, and Ebony, but they weren't interested and soon buggered off. Bloody clueless if you ask me."

"Okay mate, are you settled for the night? Enough food and beer?"

"Yeah, we've got the lot. Tank is expecting a call from Jasmin tonight, so maybe some news. Anything important I'll give you a bell. We'll be round in the morning for coffee."

"Okay, good."

21—The artist amongst us

Begonia strolled in with bags that smelled good. She angrily expressed her thoughts in Basque about the sisters and their excessive jewellery. "Eneko, it must be worth a fortune, unless it's made of glass, but it's not."

I went and washed before slipping into the bath while the girls caught up with the day's events. They got washed and climbed into the bath; time to relax. They got out first and start preparing the food while I stayed put in the bath. The girls were in an excellent mood: George because she'd helped Viv and family. And Begonia because she'd got the sisters to come along to the warehouse tomorrow. The dinner was superb, and so was the wine. Begonia was showing us her culinary skills, wonderful.

George said, "Wonderful nosh Bee, why don't you show Eneko your sketches?"

Begonia gave George a proper look and shook her head.

"Sketches," I said?

George disappeared into the flat and came back with a leather A3 art portfolio. Begonia didn't look happy at all and tried to stop George from opening the portfolio, but didn't stand a chance. Begonia had another rant in Basque and stamped her foot. This appeared to be a new vulnerable side to Begonia. George spread a few sketches out on the table. The first one was a reclining naked Rhian in a basket chair in her cottage in Wales. The second was of George sitting on the edge of the bath brushing her hair. Begonia had caught her muscular frame perfectly. The third was a naked Jasmin, having her long hair brushed by a naked George. All of them were splendid, and she had used the charcoal shading skilfully.

"Begonia, these are excellent sketches. You must concentrate on doing more work like this. People will queue up to have their portraits by you."

"Eneko, not everybody wants other people to see themselves revealed, warts and all. Would you pose naked for me?"

"I'll think about it, but you have lots of other options: people love their portraits, either in charcoal, watercolours, or oils. You must make the most of your talents."

"Told you." Chimed in a beaming George.

"Begonia, when you have time, I'll commission you to sketch all our staff, and we'll put them up on the wall in the reception. Better make it head and shoulders only, don't want to frighten the clients."

"Eneko, that's nice. I'll do it soon. I'm thinking of going to the washhouse and doing some sketches there. Do you think the ladies will mind?"

George said, "I'll go with you. They'll love it. And I know Vee would love to have you sketch her."

"I'll take my camera with me and then, for the group scenes, I can work off the photos. It'll be quicker that way and more honest."

"I can develop them for you, so no need for added expense."

"Okay boss, we're off to bed. See you bright and early in the morning. I'll come round and get the coffee going."

George grabbed the portfolio, kissed me on the cheek, Begonia gave me a big hug and a kiss, "Eneko, you're good for my ego."

I stayed up for a while, running options through my head. I needed to think and use the meditation techniques I'd learnt in Japan. Sometimes I wondered if I had ever been to Japan and learnt martial arts and became an efficient and quite ruthless fighter. I had another woman to thank for that, Yua. She had tutored me in some many things, but she had encouraged me to face my demons and to do something positive about them. Would she be happy about how it turned out? I slept well and woke to the smell of coffee and croissants. George was already in the office. After dressing, I wandered into the office. George said, "Morning En, coffee?"

Nodding, I sat down and buttered my croissants and drank my coffee. The phone rang, George answered, "Oh hi Tank, yeah, the coffee is on the boil and toast is almost ready. See you soon."

"En, Bee has gone to the office and then she's going to the Adelphi and taking the sisters to see the warehouse at 10 am."

"Good. We'll get an update from Tank and Binns and then set our plan in motion."

Chapter 22—Transporting drugs

Tank and Binns arrived. "Morning George, the coffee smells good, better than Tank's effort this morning."

Tank spoke, "I had a long chat with Jasmin last night and she thinks I need to talk to her sisters about their current actions and the likely repercussions, she thinks they're clueless and just think they are in control when in fact they're not. Jasmin thinks we should lay it on the line and persuade them to live in France and Mr Daud will provide them with an income so they can live a decent lifestyle, but also be prepared to work!"

Binns nodded. So did George and me.

"We must persuade the sisters to disappear before the mob gets its hands on them, then we can concentrate on sorting them out, with the help of the law. When Begonia meets them and brings them to the warehouse, we intercept them and take them to Wales, and Mr Daud can have a long chat with them."

Binns asked what was on everyone's lips: "Do we know why the mob wants the warehouse?

"It's got to be drugs, Binns, just like the case with Charlotte."

The phone rang, George answered it, said little, just, "Okay, tomorrow at 10 am."

"That was a solicitor, he wants to see Bee tomorrow, something about a will!"

"Okay, Tank, you're in charge of dealing with the mob. Binns, you get the sisters to Wales, and I'll have a word with Sugar and find out what he knows. George, you come with me, and we'll watch Tank's back."

Everybody left. George put on some coffee and lit up a couple of Passing Cloud. "What do you reckon, George?"

"I think you're right. The sisters must owe the mob a bundle and they won't take no for an answer, but I don't think they're here for the air. It's money, and that means drugs. Do you think they want to use the warehouse as a distribution centre for their drugs? It would make sense, but the drugs would need to be ready to go. They wouldn't be able to cut or do whatever they do with them at the warehouse. It would all need to be packaged and boxed before it reached the warehouse."

"George, I agree, so where do the drugs come from? The answer is the docks, but that would take a big operation. I wonder if Geoff, Charlotte's old flame, has heard anything? I'll give him a ring later."

George grabbed her coat. I did likewise. "Gun?" I asked. She nodded.

We walked up the lane arm in arm, just a couple out for a stroll. As we entered the street, we could see Tank chatting with three blokes. We stopped by the telephone box, and I waited outside while George made an imaginary call. Nobody took any notice of us and Tank took them through to the office. We waited, after about 10 mins they came out. Shook hands with Tank and walked up to the top of the street. Tank wandered down to us.

"Interesting. They want us to handle merchandise from the docks and deliver it to five centres across the country. So, it's a piece of cake, and the money would be good, too good, in fact!"

George smiled. "I can see a certain policeman being interested in this latest development."

"Yeah, but let's hang fire until the sisters have a chat with Mr Daud."

At 10 am, Begonia got out of a taxi with the sisters and went into the warehouse. After about 30 minutes, Binns arrived, and the sisters got into the Land Rover and Binns drove off. Begonia came out, waved and said she was going back to the office. George looked at me and we entered the warehouse to meet Tank.

"What just happened, Tank?" George asked.

"It was weird. I started talking to them in the office and I was going to talk to them about the danger they were in when the phone rang. It was Jasmin. The entire conversation was in their language, with some

French thrown in. They looked shocked and terrified. Jasmin said she's going to ring us at your office in ten minutes and explain everything."

We hurried back to the office. George started making coffee when the phone rang. I motioned for Tank to answer it. "Yes, it's me. What just happened to your sisters?"

He listened for a while and then said, "Call me tonight at 10 pm."

George raised both eyebrows. Tank laughed. "Those gangsters have just had the fear of God put into them. They know we have the upper hand as well as the ruby. They know Jasmin is safe with us. The sisters listened to Jasmin, who was very harsh with them, and told them if they didn't go to France and agree to Mr Daud's terms, they were on their own. They grabbed the deal with both hands. They don't know what they're doing. Jasmin said Mr Daud will escort them to Paris tomorrow and then return to Liverpool in a couple of days."

"Excellent, well done, Tank and Jasmin, of course. That just leaves the drug runners. Can't wait. I'll have a quick chat with Geoff and see if he knows anything."

I rang Geoff. Not pleased to hear from me after our last meeting at Charlotte's house, but he answered all my questions. A new crew dealing in the drug trade had a lab onboard their ship and did all the work at sea and unloaded in port. No doubt the usual bribes, etc., being paid. I relayed the information, it all fit. I needed to discuss this piece of news with Sugar.

Tank said, "See you later. I've got a few things to get ready before Jasmin comes over to the flat. Why don't we all meet up here tomorrow at lunch?"

"Sounds good. Tank, George and I have got some planning to do as well. If Binns rings, let him know what we're up to."

Tank waved and sauntered off. George looked at me, "Plenty of time for a workout before Bee gets back and then bath time for clean bodies and logical minds."

Begonia returned at 6 pm and had a bath. I was daydreaming, and they were talking about the Goon Show of all things and how difficult some of the humour was for Begonia, which surprised me. Then George said, "Bee, I've just remembered a solicitor rang for you this morning and wants you to go to his office at 10 am tomorrow. I've left the name and address on the desk."

"A will?

"Yeah, a will."

"I do not know what that's about, but no doubt I'll find out in the morning."

George and I had not come up with any ideas, so we called it a night and went to bed. The incessant ring of the phone interrupted my dreams. I glanced at the clock—4 am. I picked up the phone.

Rabbit said, "Eneko, Mr Daud, and the sisters are taking the early flight from Ringway, Binns is driving but we have a problem: as they came past, I noticed two cars moving out to follow them and one of them I recognised from the raid at the cottage."

"Not to worry Rabbit, Tank and I will get on it right away. I'll call you later."

I rang Tank, "It's Eneko. Have you got your car ready to fly? Binns is driving to Ringway for the early-bird flight to Paris and Rabbit reckons he's being followed."

"Give me 5 minutes. See you at your front door."

The Zephyr came to a halt, and I jumped in. "Binns will go via Northwich and Knutsford, so if we move it, we can go through the tunnel and intercept them before they reach anywhere near the airport. I think they'll wait for a clear stretch of road with minimal traffic, most likely near Delamere Forest."

Tank hit the accelerator, and we raced through the tunnel and headed for Northwich, the headlights blazing. Tank soon had the car zipping along. Dawn would soon break, so speed was essential. I started checking my guns. Tank handed me his, so I checked that as well. So far, so good, and so little traffic on the road. We reached the A556, and I hoped we had got ahead of them. Tank slowed, and we watched as the dawn broke. Nothing ahead of us on the road, so maybe we had got lucky. We drove on for about 20 minutes. We were both getting anxious when Tank said, "I've got Binns in my mirror, Eneko."

"Okay, let him go past. He'll recognise your car and take off. We'll give those idiots something to think about."

Binns swept past. I motioned for him to move it, which he did. The two cars tried to do the same until I opened up with my gun, the bullets crashing into the headlights and bonnet. The first car swerved to the side of the road and ran up the bank. Tank screamed to a halt and both of us opened fire on the second car, which swerved and ran into a ditch. Tank swung the car around and we drove past the wreckage. The idiots were dragging themselves out of their cars. Tank put a few rounds into the front tires of both cars, and we raced off.

"A lovely morning for a drive, eh? Eneko."

"Perfect, Tank, and plenty of time to get back for breakfast."

Chapter 23—The new girl

Tank dropped me off at the office. He was heading back to check on things at the warehouse. I entered the office to the smell of coffee and voices! George was there and was chatting to a young woman with long red, curly hair, a very slim frame, and an engaging smile.

"Morning Eneko, you're up early," said George. "This is our new secretary, Viv."

"Hi Viv, George has told me so much about you, pleased to have you onboard."

"Morning, Mr Sora, it's lovely to meet you. I hope I won't let you down."

"I'm sure you won't, but you answer to George, not me."

"En, I'm just going up to my place to show Vee a few things, then we'll be right back, okay?"

"Take your time. I'm not out until 11:30 am."

The girls left, and I rang Sugar to confirm our meeting in the White Star at 11:30 am. His secretary said he was out, but he'd got the appointment in his diary. I sat by the phone, waiting for a call from Binns. The door opened and in walked George and behind her, Viv. George said, "What do you reckon to our new secretary?"

"Wow, Viv, you look like the perfect secretary. I love the outfit. It's smart."

"God! My kids won't recognise me."

The phone rang. George motioned to Viv. "Good morning, Mr Sora's office, Vivian the secretary speaking. Yes, he is. I'll put him on now."

George and Viv were beaming and trying hard not to laugh. I picked up the phone. The dulcet tones of Sugar emerged. "Another secretary, mate. I hope George is still in charge?"

"Most definitely. Are you at the White Star already? Okay, give me five minutes?"

I smiled at the girls, and got to go, "You look and sound the part, Viv."

"Why thank you, Boss."

I ambled up to the White Star. Sugar was already on a pint of the black stuff and accompanied by a uniformed sergeant who was enormous, as tall as Sugar but about twice as wide. Maisy was serving and beaming like a Cheshire cat. "The usual En?"

I nodded. Sugar grabbed me by the shoulder, Eneko. "May I introduce you to my new sergeant, Patrick Murphy?"

"Delighted to meet you, sergeant."

"I'm delighted to meet you, Eneko. Mr Shaw has told me all about you."

"All good, I hope?"

"Mums the word, Eneko."

I laughed. He was likeable. He looked about 50 and his face carried a few scars but also a wide smile. I took an instant liking to him, but I wouldn't like to get the wrong side of him.

"Business is looking good with a new secretary, eh, mate? Crime pays, eh sergeant?"

"I wouldn't quite say that sir, but sometimes it has a head start."

We got down to business. I told Sugar and the sergeant what I'd gathered about the London gangs and how I thought the drugs came into the country and got distributed. They looked at me but didn't say a word. I also mentioned that I'd got number plates and photographs of most of the villains. The sergeant and Sugar both looked impressed. But before they could say anything, Maisy interrupted, "En, there's trouble at the mill."

Sugar was out of the door before me, and we were both followed by Sergeant Murphy. As we rounded the corner to the office, we could see George punching at a spiv who had a cosh and looked like he knew how to use it. Sugar arrived and wrenched the cosh out of his grasp.

"Who's this, George?"

"Viv's useless ex tried to get some money off her and when she refused, because she has got none, he tried to beat her up."

Sugar glared at him. "Any reason I don't bounce you up and down the lane for laughs, pal?"

Sergeant Murphy interrupted, "Excuse me sir, I think there's been a bit of a misunderstanding here. Why don't I and the young fellah go for a walk and have a chat like. I'm sure we can sort out the problem."

George looked like she was about to thump him, but Sugar said, "Okay, Sergeant Murphy, we'll be in the office when you've finished talking."

In the office, Viv had gone to the bathroom, George went to see how she was. She came out and said Vee's got a black eye and a cut lip, but she'll be out soon.

"Any coffee going, George?" Said Sugar.

George looked at him, "Yes sir, right away," before giving him a kiss on the cheek.

Sugar was beaming. "The Remy smells good, too."

George said, "Sugar, you have the nose of a bloodhound."

Viv came out of the bathroom, looking very embarrassed and with a real blackeye. Sugar went over, sat her down on the sofa. "Now Viv, don't you be worrying at all, my Sergeant is Irish, and he's got a fine way with the English language. He'll sort the problem out in a jiffy."

"Are the kids in school I asked?"

George said, "Yeah, and with their school uniforms on, they looked really smart."

"Kids?" Said Sugar.

"Yeah, I've got twins, one of each, 7-year-olds."

Sugar nodded. "I'll just see what's holding up my sergeant. He's already got lost a few times, as he only arrived in Liverpool last weekend."

George raised her eyebrows and looked madder than hell. I said, "George, why don't you show Viv the new extension to your apartment?"

George got the hint and took Viv with her. I started pouring the coffee just as Sugar and Sergeant Murphy arrived back. Sugar looked at me and winked, "Sergeant Murphy had a word, and it seems the lad agreed that his best course of action is to live in London otherwise the drugs and revolver we found on his person may come to light if he ever steps foot in our fair city again."

"Brandy with your coffee, sergeant?"

"Most kind, Eneko."

"Right, Eneko, let's get down to the proper business at hand. We'll check what we can. I'll take the photos with me and get back to you tonight. Sergeant Murphy will get a team together and check out the shipping links and see if we can come up with a couple of likely leads. Get George to have a word with Viv and tell her not to worry, her ex won't be back, just get on with her life. She looks sound, Eneko and good you've got the kids in school. Stay alert. We'll talk soon."

They left. The sergeant gave me a huge wink. I heard George saying goodbye and then the girls came back into the office.

Viv put her new door key on the desk, walked over to me and kissed me. "You're a lovely man, Boss. You can depend on me. I'll never let you down. I can't believe my luck. I can't wait for the kids to come home and see the flat. They'll be over the moon."

I looked at Viv. She looked as honest as the day was long. She looked at home in the office. It felt right. I smiled, "Remember, George is your real boss."

George hooted, "Yeah right."

I left them to it and disappeared for a coffee at the Kardomah and the chance to put the persistent wave of doubt that was troubling me to bed. I was getting nowhere with my current train of thought when

Ruby appeared with my coffee and a piece of paper, which she put in my hand, "From Geoff," she said.

She carried on serving, and I looked at the paper. One word: SS Magellan. I was more than surprised. Ruby appeared again with another coffee. I raised an eyebrow. She pointed and Begonia came in and deposited herself at the table.

"Eneko, you won't believe what happened! I went and saw the solicitor and he gave me a letter from Charlotte. The letter was strange. She apologised for getting us involved in the drugs and sex parties in Hong Kong and Liverpool and said she'd always admired us and treasured our friendship. And it was payment for her husband's cruelty. The solicitor then showed me a part of her Will and Testament in which she'd left her cottage in Wales to me and her house in Chester to Kimiko. All the rest went to her brother. He was happy for Kimiko and me to receive the houses, so it's all settled. I now own a place in Wales near your place and George's!"

"Jesus, we're building an empire out in Wales. George will be over the moon!"

"I know, okay I'm off to the office. Got to sort something out this afternoon for Senor Bengoa. See you after work."

I walked down to the Pier Head to clear my thoughts. The sun was out, it was warming up. A bunch of dockers came past heading for the tram, the smell of unwashed bodies awaiting their Sunday bath wafted past. School kids adorned with blackheads and hair full of brylcreem sauntered past, heading for the ferry. As did the scuff-shoed office workers with their shiny, threadbare suits and nicotine-stained fingers. This was life in Liverpool, tough but real. I headed back to the office. I couldn't wait to see the look on George's face when Begonia came up with the news of her inheritance. I arrived as the twins did, Eric with his tie eschew and his cap on backwards, but he looked happy.

"Right said Viv, you two come with me, we've got things to do."

"But what about my lesson with George?"

"Later, son, now get a move on. See you in the morning, boss."

George said, "I've given Vee a week's pay in advance so she can get set up. Is that okay?"

"George, you know it is. I think you've done a superb job. Viv is a find."

The door flew open, Begonia came in with bags of shopping. "We're celebrating tonight, after I've had a bath. Come on, George, move your arse."

Before George could utter a word, the bags were in the kitchen and Begonia had the bath on and said, "Come on George, let's get some towels and a change of clothes."

I had a shower in the apartment and left them to take a bath. I was feeling peckish, so I looked in the bags, lots of goodies and Champagne, which I put in the fridge. I poured myself a drink of a chilled white wine when I heard whoops and laughter from the bathroom. There was a knock on the door. I answered and Viv came in. More laughter erupted from the bathroom, followed by a naked Begonia and George. George yelled, "Vee, this is Bee and we're going to have some Champagne. Why don't you join us?"

Viv laughed and said, "I've just got to go back to the flat with Eric's school book. Frank is around, so no doubt he'll look after the twins. Give me 5 minutes."

Begonia said, "Who's that? She's gorgeous."

George laughed. "She's our new secretary as of today."

"Girls, maybe put some clothes on and I'm starving."

"Okay En, but what about the news? More scousers in Wales, brilliant?"

The champagne chilled; the girls clothed, and we were just waiting for Viv. Begonia was busy with the food and George had put on some of my jazz when Viv returned. Begonia started talking to her ninety to the dozen while serving food. George was laughing. I opened the champagne, and we drank to the new team and, of course, to Begonia's inheritance. Viv looked like she was enjoying herself and didn't appear fazed by the girls' talk of property and fashion. Begonia was up on her feet with Viv standing back-to-back and Begonia saying they were the same height and build, although Vee looked thinner.

George said, "Bee, what about that stuff that doesn't fit you anymore and some of Kimi's gear?"

"Of course, George, why didn't I think of that? Come on girls, let's try on some clothes."

The girls went off to the apartment, and I ruminated about the job at hand. It had all gone quiet, too quiet. But I now had the ship's name in my pocket and the law on my side in Sugar, and our own kind of law with Binns, Tank, George, and myself. I realised I hadn't heard from Tank or Binns. I rang the apartment at the warehouse, "Tank, it's Eneko, everything okay?"

"Yeah, all good. Binns and Jasmin have just arrived. We got delayed a bit."

"We're having a bit of a get-together at the office. If you and Jasmin want to meet our new secretary and have a drink, just for a while, then you can get back to the flat."

Tank laughed, "Yeah, see you in five minutes."

Tank, Binns, and Jasmin arrived, and I was just pouring some champagne when the three musketeers entered with a flourish of colour and swirling skirts. The girls introduced Viv, and they all started talking fashion. Tank and Binns looked at me and we left them to it and slid off to the White Star. Maisy pulled a couple of pints and a dry sherry for me. Maisy said to me, "That sergeant is a real hunk. I love a big man. Maggie was smitten, big enough for both of us, I reckon." Then licked her lips and gave me a wink. I followed the boys into the snug at the back, in the back, and out of the way. I slid the piece of paper with the name of the ship over to them. "What's that?" Said Binns.

"I think it's the name of the ship that they bring the drugs into port. I'm going to check with Sugar tomorrow and see if it fits into his investigation. If so, we may be on their trail."

Binns looked at us. "Cheers lads, I must be getting old. I didn't see those idiots following me earlier. I think you stopped a bloodbath."

"Tank drove like a pro, and nobody got hurt on our side. But let's have a think about it and get together for lunch tomorrow, okay?"

Tank said, "Jasmin's got an interview for a job at the Royal next week, so need all this sorted out by then. She reckons Mr Daud will be back in a few days. He'll ring Jasmin to let her know. Jasmin says he's got contacts in France, so she doesn't see any problems."

We walked up the lane together. Jasmin and George were talking in the office. Jasmin got up and gave George a hug, kissed me and Binns on the cheek and said see you later.

Chapter 24—Lover's tiff

George looked a bit put out. "What's up?"

"Bee and Vee have gone up to the apartment, Bee showed Vee the sketches of me, and Vee couldn't wait to have her sketch done. They're up in the apartment now, posing and drawing!

"So what?"

"I think Bee fancies Vee and by the look on Vee's face, the feeling is mutual. I think men come way down on the list with Vee and to be honest, I'm not surprised her experience of men is awful. She told me that her ex used to beat her up when she was young and then rape her when she refused to have sex with him. It's only now that she's had the courage to stand up to him and now, they'll be no stopping her."

"George, slow down. It's just an infatuation. Begonia feels like an elder sister, a bit like you do, I expect."

"I bloody well hope so. I don't know what to do now. Do I go back and interrupt the sketching or what? I feel like a spare prick at a wedding."

"George, just wander back. It's your place. Just be nice and say the right things, okay?"

"Suppose you're right. See you for breakfast."

Time for some Django, so I poured myself a Remy and tried to relax.

Light was trying to enter the bedroom. The radio, the noise of the coffee machine, and George's singing dragged me to full consciousness. I got dressed and headed into the office. George beamed at me, poured me a coffee, and lit me a Passing Cloud. "Croissant, En?"

"Love one. You look chipper this morning?"

"Feel it. Bee's sketch of Vee is coming on. Wait until you see it."

The office door opened and in came Viv, "Morning, all."

She kissed George on the cheek and sat down.

"Coffee, Vee?"

"Please, and then can you tell me what you want me to start on with today?"

"Sure, just give me a minute. Did you enjoy sitting for Bee last night?"

"Sitting, I loved it. I do a bit of sitting at Liverpool Art College when they need someone skinny. The money is fantastic. The sketch looks good so far, don't you think?"

George laughed. "I think it looks lovely. I'm sure the boss would love to see it."

"I love art, especially naked women."

Viv laughed, "Typical man, eh George?"

The phone rang, Viv answered it, and mouthed, "Are you in, it's Sugar?"

I nodded. Viv passed me the phone. "What's up?"

"I thought I'd catch up and see what's going on."

I said, "I've got the name of a ship, the SS Magellan."

"Right, you lovely man, I'll do a check right now. Call you later."

The phone rang again. Begonia whispered, "Can we meet for coffee now at the Kardomah and don't tell George it's me?"

I said, "See you in 5 minutes, sir."

George looked at me. "A client maybe. See you later."

Begonia was sitting at the back of the cafe; Ruby caught my eye and brought me over a coffee and another one for Begonia. "What's up?"

The reply came in Basque like "What's up? It's that bloody bitch of a partner of yours. She was crazy in bed last night."

"Begonia, I don't want to know about your love life."

"Ah, you should. You may be minus a partner soon, look." She moved, so she had her back to me, and raised her skirt, no underwear but a very red rear end that looked quite bruised and painful.

"I can't sit down, she spanked me, she knows I like it but no way that hard, she's a real bitch."

She had tears in her eyes. I took her hands in mine. "Begonia, you know George is mad about you. I think she just got jealous of you paying lots of attention to Viv."

"Viv! Viv loves art. We talked about art. She sits in the live class at the college, that's all."

"I know, but I think George got the wrong end of the stick. I'll have a word with her today, and I'm sure things will be back to normal this evening."

She kissed me on the cheek. "Thank you, Eneko, but George is going to have a sore arse tomorrow."

I laughed. She smiled and stood up. "See you later."

Ruby gave me a quizzical look as I paid the bill and said, "Some people have all the luck."

I left and wandered back to the office. George was on the phone and Viv was typing up a storm. George put the phone down. "That was Sugar. He said he'll see us in the White Star in about half an hour."

"Okay, let's go now. I'm thirsty. Hold the fort, Viv, if you need us at the pub, the number is on the sheet by the phone."

"Okay boss, enjoy lunch."

As we entered the White Star, Maisy waved and pointed to the back room. "The usual she mouthed." George nodded.

We sat at the table facing the door. Maisy brought the drinks over, looked at my face, and departed without a word.

"George, you are going to be nice to Begonia tonight. She showed me her arse this morning. It's bruised as hell. What the hell got into last night? You know she's nowhere near as physical as you or as tough."

"Where did she show you, her arse?"

"In the bloody Kardomah, she was in tears. You better sort it out tonight. I'll put the herbs and lincture on the side of the bath, so all you have to do is bathe her and then take her to bed and be nice."

George looked like she was about to burst into tears. "George, no bloody tears. Sugar is going to appear in a moment, and it'll be business as usual, okay?"

"I'm just going to the ladies, back in 5 minutes."

Maisy arrived with a pint of the black stuff, gave me a look, "Is George, okay?"

"Yeah, she's fine. Just got a bit of a headache."

I got another look for that statement, but before she said anything else, Sugar arrived. "Morning Eneko, that information looks like it may be gold. I've checked out the ship and it looks dodgy, too few ports for a tramp steamer. Did you have any luck with the warehouse owners and what they said?"

"Yeah, Tank is acting as overall manager for Senor Bengoa, and he gave them a price and they seemed okay with it. They said they would be in touch in a few days. So, maybe we could do a combined operation and get two birds with one stone."

"Could do. The ship is due to dock tomorrow night or the following morning. That gives us time to get something sorted. I got a line on some more dodgy looking villains. They're from the smoke, so eyes open. Oh! Did you hear about two cars getting shot up, three villains injured, cars out of commission, and nobody saw anything? The news is they were all from the smoke."

"No, heard nothing."

Binns and Tank appeared, "Who got shot, Sugar?"

"Just a couple of idiots from the smoke. How are you guys doing? Eneko and I have just been talking about you two and the warehouse. Any news on the new business?"

Tank replied, "Just got the word. That's why we're here. They want to drop the stuff off in a few days. They want to know if we can transport it over the weekend. They want it moved without delay."

"Brilliant, now we're talking. Hi George, didn't know you were here. How's things with my second favourite lady in the world?"

George laughed, "Morning all, Sugar, your 2nd favourite girl is fine and curious about recent developments."

"Well, let's see what pans out in the next few days. I've got to be somewhere else soon, so I'll love you and leave you. Let's talk soon."

We finished our drinks and headed on our separate ways, Binns and Tank, to make sure everything was okay at the warehouse and the lorries on standby for the incoming shipment. I headed back to the office with George. She had little to say and went straight back to work with Viv, sorting out a couple of things we were going to look at in the next week. The afternoon passed; the twins came racing in. Eric to announce he had some cars to wash at Frank's and Helen to say she had finished her latest drawing at school. George and Viv looked impressed, so was I. It looked bright and cheerful; Begonia would be over the moon as she had been helping Helen to draw.

Viv said to George, "If Bee wants me to sit tonight I can, but if she's busy not to worry. I've got a job tomorrow at the college after work, so I'm not available until the weekend."

"I'll tell Bee when she gets back and let you know."

After Viv left, George looked at me. "I messed up last night. What should I do?"

"Get the bath ready, the herbs are in place, get a nice big fluffy bathrobe and be yourself. I've put a nice bottle of rose in the fridge. Why not take it into the bathroom and make a night of it?"

The phone rang. Geoff said, "Was the information any good?"

"Hi Geoff, yes, I think so. I'll let you know how it goes in a few days. Just stay out of sight."

"Will do, take care."

The office door opened and in came Begonia, looking a mite tired. I said, "George has got the bath going. Why don't you jump in and relax? You'll feel a lot better." George came out of the bathroom and hugged Begonia. I said, "Just nipping off to the White Star for a pint."

In the pub, Maggie was tending bar. "Alright Eneko, what can I get you?"

"A large brandy, thanks." Maggie went to get a bottle when Maisy nodded to her and produced a bottle of Remy from under the counter and poured me a very large one.

I smiled and said, "Cheers ladies." I wandered into the snug and tried to put my thinking cap on. Maisy ambled over, lit me a Passing Cloud, "Is George, okay?"

"Yeah, she had a falling out with Begonia, but they're okay now. I've just left them to it."

"Why don't you make George an honest woman? Girl stuff is okay, but it doesn't get you anywhere in the long run, En, you mark my words."

I smiled, "You are a woman of experience, then?"

"Not really, but I know what's going on."

She left me to my thoughts. After I'd finished my drink, I returned to the office. A voice rang out, "Eneko, come and get in the bath. It's lovely."

I went into the bathroom, washed myself, and climbed into the bath. The girls were smiling. George had cleared the air. Begonia stood up. "Does my arse look better?"

"Better than what?"

"Better than this morning?"

"It looks a lot less raw and I'm sure by tomorrow you'll be feeling much better."

They had been drinking, the bottle of rose was empty. Begonia's face was flushed. She said, "Eneko, can I ask you a question? How come you don't get horny? Loads of women would jump into bed with you in a heartbeat."

"Bee, don't be nosy, En is his own man, and he doesn't need lectures on his total lack of sex life from us." They laughed, oh how they laughed.

"Begonia said, "Eneko, why don't you take Viv out? She thinks you're cute and I bet she's a tiger in bed."

"Thank you, ladies, 'tis past my bedtime. See you in the morning."

"I'll do a sketch of you and show Viv, perfect plan."

I left them to it and wandered into my flat, dried off and put on some music and tried to relax. I soon drifted off and awoke to the smell of coffee and bacon.

George was smiling to herself and frying the bacon. I walked up behind her and patted her arse.

"Jesus, Eneko, be gentle. Bee got her own back this morning, but no more. I've broken that bamboo cane and thrown it in the bin."

"So, all's well, then."

"Look, sorry about us teasing you last night. We shouldn't have. But you worry me, you know."

"Thanks for caring, but I'm alright, okay?"

"Good, because I think tonight could be our last quiet night, so we're making dinner at 7:30 pm sharp."

Chapter 25—The Artist at work

The day passed. No mad phone calls or death threats from London-based gangsters. Viv and George worked away all day. They seemed to get on well. The twins arrived at 4 pm. Eric shot off straight away to see Uncle Frank and Helen sat down and carried on drawing. The twins were nothing like each other. George said, "Vee, let's call it a day. We've done loads, see you in the morning, and you, Helen, kiss time." Helen grinned and gave George a kiss on the cheek, and then they were gone.

George smiled. "I'll put the bath on. Let's close and do an hour of practice before Bee gets home."

We worked hard on lower body strength and kicks to the knee and ankles. Followed by some upper body stuff with weights. George looked the part, and she was getting strong. Her bench presses and squats were excellent. We finished up and got back to the office just as Begonia arrived. She had bags of groceries with her and some wine. While I got washed and sat in the bath, the girls came in, got washed and as George was getting into the bath, Begonia pretended to give George a slap on the rear end, but didn't and just winked at me. The conversation was about the local news and Begonia telling us she'd signed up for a course at the Art College, a lunchtime course three times a week studying water colours. We got out of the bath and got dried, the girls into fluffy dressing gowns. Begonia said, "I need you naked, Eneko. I'm sketching you, so recline on the couch, please. And no, I'm not taking no for an answer. You can concentrate on the wonderful aromas coming from George's cooking."

I was about to raise my complaints when George mouthed, "Please, En."

So, I reclined. After 20 minutes, Begonia passed me a glass of wine and said, "You can have a drink. I've got the main outline. You may have to remain stationary now and again, though."

Begonia kept glancing at me and seemed very professional. George looked over her shoulder now and again and gave me the thumbs up. I suffered in silence, and it seemed to go on forever. George sang out, "Dinner is ready."

"Can I put some clothes on, Begonia?"

"Put on your dressing gown. I'll need you naked again after dinner, not for long, so don't be stroppy."

Dinner was superb, as was the wine. I was enjoying the girls' banter. Everything was back to normal, thank God. Begonia said, "Okay, Eneko, get naked again. It won't take long now."

I must have dozed off because as I opened my eyes, Begonia and George were looking at the sketch, but so was Viv. "Ah! The sleeping beauty awakes, so what do you think, girls, a perfect likeness?"

Viv said, "It's wonderful Bee, I can't wait to see the finished portrait."

George said, "Fantastic, but his John Thomas is bigger than that, sometimes anyway." They all burst out laughing.

I said, "You're all fired, including the artist."

George handed me my dressing gown. "Come and have a look. It's very good."

Begonia put the sketch on the table, and we all gathered around. It looked professional. Begonia was a talented artist.

I looked at Viv. "You've seen mine; can I see yours?"

They all laughed, and Begonia opened her portfolio case and took Viv's sketch out. She had finished it. It looked wonderful. Viv looked flabbergasted.

"Bee, wow, that's superb. Nobody has ever caught me like that. I'm delighted." And she gave Bee a big kiss on the cheek.

And I followed. "Begonia, I love it. These portraits are part of the commission I mentioned."

George looked very proud of Begonia. "I think this deserves a toast, girls, and I went and grabbed a bottle of bubbly out of the fridge."

Viv said, "And I only popped down because I'd forgotten to get milk."

George chipped in, "A glass of bubbly and a look at the boss's best bits, not bad, eh!" We all laughed and settled down to have a drink, but Viv swigged hers and said, "See you in the morning, no cocoa for the kids means no sleep."

The evening ended, and the girls had an early night. I slept well and was up early training, soon followed by George. We had a hectic session, and we even managed some target practice with the guns. George loaded the weapons. Both of us were in the office for only a few moments before Viv arrived. She made the coffee and toast. The phone rang. "Viv speaking, just a moment, Sugar. I'll pass the phone over to him."

"Eneko, the ship is docking tonight at the Albert Dock, a change of plan. I've got my lads all ready and primed to go tomorrow morning around 8 am, plenty of light so we can see who we're after. It's not likely to be a huge load, but I'm sure it'll be hard to locate."

"Yeah, it seems to be a very easy target. That's what worries me. Okay, I'll get Tank and Binns at the warehouse up to speed and then we'll see where it goes."

A knock at the door and Tank came in, "Morning all." George and Viv beamed at him, and George said, "Coffee Tank?"

Chapter 26—The Wapping Tunnel

"Yeah great, thanks, George. Eneko, the suspected drug guys just told me the merchandise is late. Can I organise it for the day after tomorrow?"

"That stinks, Tank. What have they got in mind, some other plan, no doubt? You know the Albert Dock is central, difficult to keep things in the dark there. How the hell would you get the goods off the dock and away without people noticing?"

Viv looked up, "Maybe use the Wapping tunnel and get it to Edgehill Station and then you could move it by rail."

Tank looked at me, "The clever bastards, well done, Viv. But do these villains have the local knowledge about the Wapping Tunnel and Edgehill? I don't, and I live here."

Viv laughed, "Well, apart from me, the actual expert is Frank. He used to work at the marshalling yards at Edgehill."

I kissed Viv on the cheek, "Brilliant, let's talk to Frank."

Tank and George, and I raced over to see Frank. He was working at his forge. "Morning, Eneko. What can I do for you?"

"Frank, have you got half an hour to tell us all about Edgehill and the Wapping Tunnel?"

"Thirty minutes. I could talk for hours about it. What do you want to know in particular?"

"Okay, if you had some cargo at Albert Dock and you wanted to spirit it away, how would you do it?"

"I'd stick it on a wagon and use the tracks under the Docker's Umbrella and get it taken through the Wapping Tunnel up to Edgehill. It's steep, but the engines do it without a hitch. Once you're at Edgehill, you can go anywhere if you've got connections and know the system. Edgehill is huge. Apart from the marshalling yards, there're the goods yard, coal bunkers, all kinds of hidey holes in the tunnels and cuttings, you could get lost there for weeks."

"Do you know anyone working at the yards who could show us the layout and maybe lend us a hand in tracing some freight?"

"Yeah, my nephew, Eddie, works there. He's a sharp lad. I could give him a ring if you like?"

"Brilliant, Frank. That could be a big help."

"Eneko, they're going to move it tonight. They must have connections and then it's gone. The deal they wanted with me was just a red herring to get us out of the way, clever bastards."

George spoke up. "We need to bring Binns up to speed and then if Frank's nephew can show us around, we are in with a chance to catch them at it. But what about Sugar? Do we tell him before or after?"

Tank replied, "After, there could be bullets and stuff flying around. Let's phone him just after we finished. He can pick up the villains and the goods. Everyone's a winner."

"I think that's for the best, Tank. Okay, let's get organised. I think it's pointless trying to stop the merchandise at the docks. We stand more of a chance at the goods yard."

Frank called, "Eneko, I've got Eddie on the blower. Have a chat with him."

"Hi Eddie, thanks for answering the call. We need some help with the layout of the station. Any chance you could show us around today?"

"Eneko, it's not a problem. I finish my shift at 6 pm. I'll meet you outside the Botanic Pub on the corner of Edge Lane and Botanic Road, Uncle Frank, will tell you, how to spot me."

"Thanks Eddie. See you later."

Frank raised an eyebrow. "Don't get my nephew into trouble, Eneko?"

"Don't worry Frank, by the way, how do I spot Eddie?"

"He has a limp—courtesy of the Normandy Landings."

Tank looked at me but said nothing. I thanked Frank and we headed over to the office. At the office, we sat down, and Viv made some coffee. Binns called and said he'd be along in 15 minutes.

George said, "Let's hope this doesn't get nasty. We need to arrive there ready for anything. They'll be armed to the teeth. Why are they using the train rather than road transport?"

Tank explained, "It's much easier to hide on a train and the police don't stop rail traffic for a stop and search. And if they've got inside help, the stuff will be hard to find."

Viv had the coffees on the table just as Binns arrived. We brought Binns up to speed. He whistled, "Clever buggers, eh! I've got the Land Rover all set up. Just need your equipment and then we're ready to go."

Viv pipped up, "I'll stay behind tonight with Begonia, so if you need anything we'll be on the phone. Frank's coming round to mine tonight, so he'll give the kids their tea and look after them."

"Good stuff, Viv. Looks like we're all set. Let's make sure we have all the equipment we need, then we can stow it away in Binns's Land Rover. What about your gear, Tank?"

"I'm all set. I can pick it up anytime. It's already checked. I just need to speak to Jasmin and tell her to stay home tonight and keep out of the way."

Binns said, "I'll run you up there now, Tank, and get your stuff and then it's just George and Eneko's gear to stow away."

George and I went into my apartment and down into the cellar. We loaded the guns, and we were ready to go. George opened her bag and took out her pistol, equipped with a silencer.

"Tank gave it to me, nice, eh!"

"No sniper rifle, then?"

"No, I think this job will be all close quarter work, don't you?"

"You're right. But there is one important point we haven't covered."

"What's that?"

"Well, Viv isn't blind, is she? Or stupid?"

"En, don't worry, I've sorted it with her. She knows it's a gym, and a darkroom just the same as I told Bee, so don't worry. Remember, she's on our side."

We went back up to the office, "You're sure you'll be alright, Viv?"

"Eneko, please don't worry. I'll stay here until you return, or I hear from you. And anyway, Bee will be here as well."

I was getting twitchy about this operation, but I kept my thoughts to myself. A toot, Binns, and Tank had arrived. George and I trooped out with our gear and got in the back of the Land Rover. It rained, and the clouds looked ominous. The light was going to be poor. Would that be to our advantage?

Binns moved off. He said, "I checked with the dock. The Magellan has already docked and is due to unload first thing tomorrow morning. I think our hunch about tonight is correct."

"Okay, so let's take a drive up to Edgehill and try to familiarise ourselves with the layout and see which ways you can get out of the yards."

We did a recce, Binns had an ordnance survey map, and was studying it while Tank drove up past Edgehill and looked for exits. We sat just outside the yard and waited for Eddie. Binns gave Tank a nod, and he drove down Botanic Road towards the pub.

As we got close, Tank stopped. "I'll check Eddie out."

Chapter 27—The Battle

Tank wandered down towards the pub and as he approached, a tall bloke wearing a raincoat and with a head of black head and a limp stepped out from the side of the pub. Tank and Eddie started talking. They exchanged smiles, a shake of hands, and then they started walking back to us. We scrunched up in the back, Tank joined, and Eddie sat in the front with Binns.

Tank introduced us all and Eddie said, "I think you're right about tonight. Something looks like it's going to happen. Two lads were hanging around and two other blokes I'd never seen before came into the shed where I work, so I pretended to be busy and grabbed some paperwork and said to the lads I was going to the main office and then calling it a day."

"So, how would they move the wagon without it being noticed?"

"Easy Eneko, they'd use a shunter, then the wagon would just roll to where they wanted it, a piece of cake, and if you've got men working for you, nobody would be the wiser."

"Okay, Eddie, how do we spot them?"

"Difficult, Eneko, but stay with me and I'll get in the marshalling yard and then we can look around. We'll have to leave the motor near the entrance and then walk over. I'll go into one of the offices that overlooks the yard. My mate's on tonight in the signal box, so no problem at all. I'll signal you with my Aldiss Lamp. Do you still remember the code, Tank?"

"Yeah, both me and Binns, so no problem."

"Okay, once I'm in, give me 20 minutes to get set up and then I'll start signalling, I'll just use directions so if anybody sees it, they won't bother."

We parked up near the main entrance and Eddie went on ahead. We stayed behind a goods train with about 30 wagons on it, so we had cover. The yard was still working. Shunters were moving wagons around to join other locomotives waiting to take their loads. The rain started lashing down. With flashes of lightning and rolls of thunder, we were getting sodden. We waited and then a light, just a few flashes and Tank said, "Let's go, it's on the northern side of the yard."

Tank went ahead with Binns. George and I kept to the left of them. The light was fading, and the ground underfoot was getting boggy. I could just about see Tank and Binns. They stopped, Tank signalled me to go further left, George came with me, and we advanced. Tank signalled again. We looked and through the gloom and rain we could see a dark-coloured van next to a wagon. The gang had the wagon door open and were carrying the cargo to the van; two others were standing guard armed with shotguns. Tank sneaked up and used a truncheon on the first one, and he went down in a heap. The other guard raised his shogun, but Binns shot him before he could get a shot off. Three more armed men came from the other side of the wagon, but they were in George's sights. The gun coughed as she fired and two of them hit the floor. I fired and shot the last in the shoulder. The van driver tried to get out and help his mates, but Binns hammered him as he got out and he hit the ground unconscious. Tank waved, and we all moved in on the wagon. We couldn't see anybody else in the incessant rain. And the thunder and lightning weren't helping. Tank and Binns threw the rest of the drugs into the van, and then we drove off. Two of the villains looked badly injured. As we came past the signal box, Eddie came out and he jumped in. "All, okay?"

"Yeah, thanks Eddie. Can we drop you off somewhere?"

"No, you're alright. I only live around the corner, just drop me off by your Rover."

Tank and I stayed in the van while George and Binns shot off in the Land Rover. I got Tank to stop by the telephone box and I dialled 999 and told them about the problem at Edgehill in my best imitation Welsh accent. We needed to dump this drug haul in plain sight of the police.

I said, "Tank, let's park the van near the police station at Cheapside and then get back to base."

He laughed, "Doing their work now, eh!" Tank drove up, and we left the van stuck against a wall with the doors open and the lights on. He jammed the horn on, and we were off. No chance of anybody seeing us in this downpour. We walked back. Tank said, "See you later when I've got dry."

Soaked, I opened the office door and Viv caught my eye, tried to say something before I got stabbed in the side; I kicked out and caught him with a vicious kick to the knee, then his friend caught me with a baseball bat, and I went down. And as I groped my way to my feet, Viv threw the coffee pot at him. He lifted the bat to smack her, and I dived over the desk to protect her and took another thump from the baseball bat. His friend slashed me twice and, as I turned to ward off the attack, I took another blow from the baseball bat. I hit the floor hard and received a kick from a steel-toed boot in the ribs and another in the testicles. I heard a shout and a couple of coughs before I blacked out.

Chapter 28-The patient

"En, En, say something!" I opened my eyes to see George. I appeared to be lying in bed. "Don't worry En, Jasmin is coming right now." I nodded.

The room seemed empty. It smelt of iodine and something else I couldn't put my finger on. I opened my eyes, my right one, the other one seemed to stay shut. I tried to raise my head, but it hurt, and a groan escaped. I heard a shout and right in front of me was George. She was holding my hand, and Jasmin was there in a white coat, looking at me. "Eneko, please don't move. You've got a lot of stitches in you, so lie still. Are you in pain?"

I looked down at my torso. It looked like a rail track with so many stitches, all red and brown from the iodine; and I could see big, black, and blue bruises on my thighs and legs. But more importantly, my testicles looked swollen as well. But no pain.

"Jesus! How long have I been like this?"

George said, "Two days, but you're going to be fine. Jasmin has done a super job with you. No broken bones, just stitches and bruises, so just relax, okay? You'll be fine."

"What about Viv and the drugs and the villains?"

"En, it's all sorted. Sugar rounded up the gang and the drugs, and we're all fine."

"How did I survive? I heard the bloody gun of yours, didn't I, George?"

Jasmin said, "Eneko, calm down."

"But what about? I didn't get another word out because Dr Jasmin stuck a needle in my arm and out I went. When I woke up, I heard voices. I was still in bed, with bits of sticking plaster on me and what looked like an ice pack on my testicles, but somehow it didn't hurt.

Jasmin and George appeared. "Coffee please, partner."

"Ah, the patient awakes, Doctor."

"Good, Eneko, you have taken a battering, but the bruises will go soon, the stitches will take longer, so you must do as you're told, okay? Maybe later today you can get out of bed for a while and move around a bit. And before you ask, your testicles are fine. The swelling and bruising is almost gone, just no excitement for a week."

"En, chance would be a fine thing, eh, Partner?"

I scowled and gave George my best pissed off look. They laughed.

"How long have I been like this?"

"This is day four," said Dr Jasmin, "And you'll need another week before the stitches come out. The internal stitches will last another day or so."

"I need to pee. Can I get up?"

"No, not yet. Nurse George will give you the bottle."

"Don't I get any privacy?"

"No, and I want to check for blood in the urine as well."

The bottle filled almost to the brim. Jasmin checked it and then smiled.

"Excellent, you're on the mend."

"En, I've got some bacon and eggs. Do you fancy some?"

"George, coffee is fine for now, honest. Can I get up for a bit, Doc?"

George looked at Jasmin. Jasmin said, "As the urine sample was fine, okay."

George got her arms under me and lifted me up on her own. I stood. It felt normal! I could feel the bruises and the blood coursing through my body. It felt

good to be alive. George and Jasmin helped me on with my dressing gown and I walked into the lounge and sat in my office chair. George brought the coffee in, and Jasmin, George, and Viv sat down, too. Before I could say anything, Viv came over and kissed me on the cheek, "Thanks boss, you saved me, you know."

"I think George saved us both. What happened to them?"

"George shot them both, not dead, and then Tank and Binns took them and dumped them at the hospital."

"What about the drugs and the gang at Edgehill?"

George spoke up. "It's all sorted. Sugar turned up at Edgehill and took charge, got them all and the geezers on the docks, plus the lab on the ship. He didn't miss a trick. The drugs were all there in the van and Sugar is now Mr Popular again. He's made sure we were never at Edgehill, impossible to see anything in the storm, anyway. I've also sorted Eddie out with some readies. Oh! Mr Daud made it to the lost property office in the Cunard Building and found his malacca walking stick with his initials on it and it had a large red ruby in the handle. Strange that."

"Well done, George. Looks like the place runs without me."

No one said a thing, just silence, then they all started laughing. I tried my best to scowl, but I couldn't manage it with my black eye. The door opened, and I caught a blast of Basque. Begonia came over and kissed me.

"Don't arouse him," said Viv.

"Don't worry, he's still on medication," said my doctor.

"Ah! That reminds me," said Begonia, and went over to the office and brought in another sketch. She opened it out. There I was, lying in bed naked, with all my stitches and bruises and with a bag of ice on my testicles. "Another one for the official office collection."

"If you think that drawing is going to be framed in the office, you can all kiss my..."

"We all did," they cooed.

About the author

As Liverpool emerged from the dust of World War 11, so did I. The birth certificate states born in Penny Lane! The years after the war and into the new decade, 1950s, were harsh. Kids with no shoes, mums with ration books, meat was sausages, butter a luxury.

My dad, an ex-Royal Marine, used to take me down to the Mersey to see the trans-Atlantic liners of the day. The buzz of the riverfront with the Liver Buildings behind and the hustle and bustle of freighters, big and small. The Overhead Railway, or the 'Docker's Umbrella', as it was known, provided a view of the entire 7 miles of docks. You could see an entire city of docks with ships coming and going to all four corners of the world—a magnificent sight.

That was the backdrop to my childhood, that and Liverpool FC. My granny lived in Lothar Road, so I used to sneak in for the last 15 mins of each game and then as I got older the Boys Pen. After School I had various jobs, then in 1965, I followed my dream of travelling the world. I started in Canada and worked there for two years, then travelled to Japan and worked there for a year. I met my Japanese girlfriend, and we travelled around SE Asia dodging the Vietnam War. After that it the heat, poverty and colour of India, and then the arid land mass of Afghanistan and Iran. Finally, Turkey and Europe. All done on a shoe-string budget.

After England I worked for 6 years in Japan, teaching English, working as a copywriter and journalist. I then moved to Spain and followed my hobby and opened a squash club which I ran for 12 years. Then marriage brought me back to the UK, where I taught and coached Squash and had two children.

Those experiences are behind the stories that I have written, with characters an amalgam of people I knew, and characters created to match the times.

Don't miss out!

Visit the website below and you can sign up to receive emails whenever David Scurlock publishes a new book. There's no charge and no obligation.

https://books2read.com/r/B-A-FNMGB-PCYKF

BOOKS 2 READ

Connecting independent readers to independent writers.

Did you love *The Malacca Umbrella*? Then you should read *The Spanish Connection*[1] by David Scurlock!

The Spanish Connection

Eneko Sora, is a private detective in Liverpool whose experiences as a journalist and his Basque heritage significantly influence his present actions. He is recovering from being stabbed and beaten in a previous case. This experience has left him with physical and emotional scars, leading him to seek rest and recuperation in Spain.

Eneko inherited his apartment in Castropol from his Uncle Jesus, a Basque sympathiser. He is fluent in Basque and is familiar with Basque culture. He feels a strong connection to his Basque roots and will help those in need, especially fellow Basques like Zoriona. This loyalty

---

1. https://books2read.com/u/bwkln0

2. https://books2read.com/u/bwkln0

extends to Sorne, his Uncle Jesus's friend, who helps him and Zoriona escape.

Eneko's personal experiences with violence and injury make him both cautious and determined in his approach to dangerous situations.

Overall, Eneko's past as a journalist and crime fighter and his personal experiences with violence have shaped him into a compassionate and resourceful individual who will stand up for what he believes in, even when it puts him in danger.

Back in Liverpool, Eneko returns to his detective work. He and his business partner, George, investigate a blackmail case involving a barrister, her secretary, and a woman named Stacey Michel. This case intersects with a wage robbery and leads them to uncover a criminal network involved in prostitution, drug trafficking, and pornography, exploiting vulnerable young girls, many of whom are orphans.

Read more at www.yamapublishing.com.

Also by David Scurlock

The Eneko Sora detective series
The Malacca Umbrella
The Spanish Connection

Standalone
The Missing Samurai Sword

Watch for more at www.yamapublishing.com.

www.ingramcontent.com/pod-product-compliance
Lightning Source LLC
Chambersburg PA
CBHW020142180626
46810CB00004B/1690